WANDA BISHOP'S
BOOK OF HOURS

SUSAN WINSHIP MCMICHAELS

ISBN 9781736937105 (paperback)

ISBN 9781736937112 (ebook)

Library of Congress Control Number: 2021906356

Published by Susan Winship McMichaels

Also by Susan Winship McMichaels

Journey out of the Garden: St. Francis of Assisi and the
Process of Individuation

The Scorpion's Helper

A PACKAGE

WANDA PULLED UP TO HER rural mailbox and rolled down the window. The mailbox was empty, except for a tiny package all the way at the back.

"Damn," Wanda muttered. She opened the car door enough to lean toward the package. The clasp on the mailbox scraped the door.

"Damn!"

Wanda cajoled the tiny package to the edge of the mailbox and put it on the passenger-side floor mat. She'd let it shed Covid until she put away her weekly curbside delivery groceries.

Wanda had made this purchase on a whim. She wanted it to bring her past to life, to help her remember when she had a life and traveled to places farther than the grocery store.

Once a year, in before times, Wanda visited the island of Manhattan.

On one long-ago visit she met her daughter at noon in Midtown near Bryant Park. Molly had secured the afternoon from her fatherly boss and would accompany Wanda to an unknown part of the island, north of the Metropolitan Museum of Art and even the Cathedral of St. John the Divine.

"You need to expand your horizons, Mom," Molly told Wanda. "This is my birthday present to you."

Wanda was touched but tried not to be effusive. She knew her existence, when too pronounced, encroached on Molly's.

After lunch in Bryant Park, Molly led Wanda to the Port Authority terminal and swiped her MTA card for their tickets up-town. Molly settled Wanda on a seat and stood guard, swaying to the rhythm of the ride. Wanda snuck admiring glances at Molly's perfect profile. Joan of Arc, she thought.

Molly's surprise was a medieval museum called The Cloisters, located in a landscape as vast and carefully planned as Central Park, but with the added attractions of hills and the Hudson River. A friend of Molly's met them at the ticket counter and explained what they should see in the time they had, which was the amount of time Molly could endure being trapped in a museum.

Molly's eyes were already glazing over.

Molly's friend gave them three manageable assignments. They were to visit a room full of unicorn tapestries, a room with glass-topped cabinets, and a Medieval garden.

Wanda's memory retained a unicorn in a small fence, Molly standing next to a pomegranate bush, and a tiny prayer book, called a Book of Hours, that once belonged to a queen of France.

Now, decades later, groceries sanitized and put away, Wanda opened the small package and settled by the fire. In her hands was a used copy of the *Book of Hours of Jeanne d'Evreux*.

The earnest introduction explained that the reproductions were enlarged, "providing as it were, an almost necessary magnifying glass for the reader." Wanda was impressed that the medieval queen had such good eyesight.

The introduction added, "To modern eyes these drollleries and grotesques must at times seem both irrelevant and irreverent in a book of prayer."

Not at all, thought Wanda. Not to me.

AMPUTATION

WANDA FELT AS IF SHE had lost a limb. Not suddenly, after a tragic accident or nasty disease. Wanda's amputation was slow and conscious and registered pain, beginning at level one, increasing gradually to ten, over five years.

It began in Mexico. Wanda was in charge of giving her sister a seventieth birthday celebration. Wanda found a yoga retreat, met her sister en route, and spent the next seven days in total sister immersion.

When they lunged, Wanda and her sister, morning and evening, in an AM hot yoga room and a PM breezy pavilion, Wanda's sister had to lift her foot with her hand and place it on the front of the mat. Wanda felt a twinge, twice a day, for the duration of the week.

But Wanda's sister also went up and down the steep mountainside to the palapa they shared, regaling Wanda with tales of trekking to Machu Picchu with a reluctant and winded lover. She led Wanda miles along a narrow trail to a beach where stoned surfers applauded as the aging sisters plunged into the waves. Wanda's sister greeted everyone they met with her perfect Spanish and then whispered her fears to Wanda. Was the man who passed them going to ambush and rape them? Did the woman ahead of them have a knife in her backpack? Which is to say, Wanda's sister behaved as oddly as she always did, at least mostly.

The only time Wanda was (blissfully) alone that week was when her sister went for a solitary swim. Wanda lay on her towel and shut her eyes. When she opened them and scanned the horizon, her sister had disappeared.

Wanda panicked and enlisted the other yogis to help. And there her sister was, (spotted by a woman with young, sharp eyes) bobbing, far out to sea. She wasn't lost. Not yet.

Now, five years later, although Wanda's sister had disappeared into death, she also stayed like some weird iteration of a phantom limb. Wanda heard her sister's voice, tired and complaining or funny and laughing. She felt her sister's neediness and anxiety. Was her sister stuck in Purgatory, trudging through drabness, on her way to eternal contentment? Would her sister be waiting for Wanda when she died? Must Wanda plod alongside her sister to Paradise?

Wanda's grandmother once counseled her to never live in the same town as her sister. Did that include Heaven or whatever the hereafter might be if it were, indeed, a something?

Wanda sat up from a painful slouch and saw an enormous woodpecker, the one with a lot of red, stealing all the food at the bird feeder. The food was intended for birds without woodpeckers' beaks, which were designed for extracting nourishing insects from trees.

Or maybe woodpeckers pecked holes in trees and the siding of houses to relieve tension, or for fun. Wanda realized this was one of the many facts she didn't know. Who was she to judge?

ANNUNCIATION

"ANY ANNUNCIATIONS?" WANDA ASKED.

Her third graders glanced from Wanda to the white board.

"Don't you mean announcements?" asked Kyle. "It's time for morning announcements."

Kyle reliably redirected Wanda whenever she strayed.

"Oh right," Wanda agreed. "But actually announcement and annunciation are synonyms. Remember synonyms?"

"Like late and tardy?" Suzie offered. "Kind of the same but different?"

"Exactly," Wanda agreed. "Tardy's a special kind of late."

"My special kind of late," said Suzie.

"Right," said Wanda.

Everyone laughed.

"Is annunciation a special kind of announcement?" Kyle asked.

Joel cleared his throat.

Here we go, thought Wanda.

"Annunciation is the angel Gabriel's announcement to the Virgin Mary that she is going to be the Mother of God."

Wanda's third graders registered this with equanimity.

Wanda, however, felt her morning getting away from her. She glanced hopefully at the clock.

"Oh," she said. "It's already time for Music. I bet you'll be singing Christmas carols."

"Christmas songs," Kyle corrected. "And Hanukah songs, and one for Kwanzaa."

"Right," Wanda said.

AT&T

Steady Humble Grateful
Steady Humble Grateful
Steady Humble Grateful

WANDA KEPT REPEATING HER MANTRA, attempting to remain calm. They told her they would call. She took them at their word, was sitting by her landline in the studio typing up a rough draft of a story, was now on page five. Still waiting for their call.

Wanda wasn't a speedy typist.

Glancing at the landline, Wanda noticed that it wasn't working. She went to the phone in the kitchen. She went to the phone by the TV. Nope. She went back to her studio and attempted to go online. No internet service.

Wanda panicked. How could they call? The sky was falling, she thought, or at least all means of communication.

Wanda breathed in (steady) and out (humble) and in (grateful). She remembered her Android. New and unfamiliar but there to rescue her, to back her up, to have her back, when all else failed. Wanda exhaled. She could call Gordon on her Android.

Yesterday, kind, befuddled Gordon at the AT&T store wanted to lower her bill, speed up her connection, and add her name to her husband's account, all to soothe the heart and mind of the frazzled old woman (does she remind him of his grandmother?) cast adrift in the world of bills and technology.

Wanda's complete mantra included, after Steady-Humble-Grateful . . . Truthful.

Wanda wasn't Truthful with Gordon when she implored him to help her. Although Wanda had only lied by misdirection, she knew full well that Gordon pictured a senile, stricken husband drooling in a recliner in front of the TV, not an exuberant escapee on a road trip in a new car headed who knows where, with the family pet. Yesterday Wanda had determined that Gordon was too young and kind and sweet for that degree of Truthful.

Wanda was impressed yesterday, in the AT&T store, by Gordon's Truthful-ness. He candidly confided that he switched his own family to a different, better communications company. Gordon agreed with Wanda that AT&T was incapable of Communication; they shared a knowing, ironic, almost cynical laugh.

Perhaps Gordon would have appreciated a Truthful portrait of Wanda's wayward husband. Perhaps today was karmic retribution.

Gordon answered the phone. He assured Wanda that Scott the Technician was on the way; AT&T's sub-contractors never called ahead. Gordon asked Wanda to call him as soon as Scott finished solving her communication problems.

Wanda sensed a coolness and a distance. Did Gordon and his grandmother have a falling out the night before?

Wanda heard a knock on the front door and reflexively missed the answering bark of the absconded family pet.

Scott was there, garrulous and beside the point. He loved Wanda's home even if the internet had to travel to it over ancient, decaying telephone lines. He feared that Gordon promised the impossible; Gordon and his kind always did. Scott allowed as how nothing could be done to improve Wanda's overpriced, underpowered, unreliable connectivity.

Wanda offered him a cookie and thanked him for his Truthful-ness.

Wanda called Gordon. Gordon ignored her calls.

Wanda ate a cookie and went for a brisk, resentful walk.

BIRD FEEDERS
AND SQUIRRELS

WANDA'S GRANDFATHER, AN ENGINEER, SCHOOLED young Wanda to explore mechanical solutions to life's problems. His yard was a maze of ingenious traps and baffles to discourage raccoons and squirrels and predatory black snakes. The creatures were largely undeterred, but Wanda's grandfather's retirement years were hopeful, and his ongoing experiments were deeply satisfying to both Wanda and him.

And so, when Wanda had her own yard and her own squirrels, she attempted to encourage their defeat through weights, levers, and in one extreme and unsporting case, a sadistic shocking mechanism with a mercifully short-lived battery. Dozens of hours were indulged in pulleys and chains precariously fixed to bars and perches jutting from trees and fence posts or, in one case, clipped to the middle of a thirty-foot wire strung six feet high between two trees.

The squirrels were patient and painstaking. Wanda imagined them with tiny clipboards taking notes and drawing diagrams. Over time, they always got the bird seed.

Finally, in her seventh decade, Wanda determined that it was time to step out of her grandfather's beloved footsteps and walk her own path, to think for herself about the habits of squirrels and the tools at her disposal.

That night, while spraying the muffin pan, Wanda had an

epiphany. Instead of anticipating corn muffins to accompany the chili cooking in the crock pot, she imagined squirrels slipping and sliding down the side of the cylindrical bird feeder, their considerable athleticism defeated by cooking spray.

Wanda's husband, her co-conspirator in dozens of years of unsuccessful squirrel abatement, looked bemused but offered no compelling counterargument. He was preoccupied with leaving Wanda.

Before he left, Wanda persuaded him to lower the bird feeder to within her reach. Wanda filled the bird feeder, sprayed it with cooking spray, and hung it on the tree. The squirrels, to their noisy and angry dismay, were thwarted from their ingenious feats and triumphs by the slippery slope.

Wanda expected they'd overcome this challenge too.

Which they did, abetted by Wanda's inconsistent application of her newest strategy. Wanda accepted this setback. Warmer weather was coming. The birds could soon fend for themselves.

Along with warming weather came a pandemic. Wanda avoided stores and embraced online shopping. The strangeness of a bag of bird seed shipped to her house was no stranger than lockdown. Still, Wanda tried to limit her exposure to strangeness with the same diligence as she limited her exposure to the virus. So, as soon as she reckoned there was plenty of free food in her yard and the woods, she stopped filling the feeder.

The squirrels rattled it indignantly for a couple of days. Then they moved on to Wanda's vegetables.

Wanda, a single adult for the first time (she married at twenty), was surprised to have to weave a global pandemic into the fabric of her new life. She had imagined volunteering and lunching with friends and sipping cocktails on people's decks. She had expected carpooling grandkids, with confidences exchanged in these brief expeditions. She had assumed hugs from her son and the other people she loved, or at least liked enough for hugging. She had planned beach time with her daughter who lived so far away.

When the weather grew cool again and the squirrels were frantic with nut collecting, Wanda carried a bag with the last of her bird seed out to the feeder. She reached up to unfasten it from the hook. It was beyond her grasp. She stood on her tiptoes. No luck. Wanda looked at the ground, wondering if the squirrels had dug a hole in the exact spot where she was standing. They hadn't.

"Damn," Wanda said to no one in particular. Actually, to herself. She, along with her life, had been shrinking.

Wanda stomped around her house. She noticed the Welcome mat. No one had been welcome in Wanda's house for months. Her husband had worn out his welcome. Then the pandemic banned all hospitality. Wanda picked up the door mat and shook it a bit. Then she carried it to the screen porch. People were still welcome on the screen porch if they wore masks and stayed six feet away from Wanda. She had marked the distance with chalk.

Wanda got the step ladder and climbed it to remove the bird feeder from its hook on a tree behind the house. She filled the feeder and then hung it on an empty plant hanger by the unused front door.

It took two days. For two days the bird feeder just hung there. Only a squirrel attempted it, unsuccessfully. But on the third day a sparrow and a blue jay darted nervously to the feeder.

By the fifth day there was a steady stream of bird traffic. You would have thought St. Francis had been rumored to put in an appearance at any moment.

Wanda could sit in the living room and watch the birds. She could sit at the dining room table and see them. And when a squirrel attempted to leap onto the feeder, she could walk out the front door and stand, arms akimbo, and glare until it slunk away.

BUILDING FIRES

THE FIRE PIT MADE NO sense. Why bundle up and shiver outside when you could sit comfortably in the house with book and lamp and sofa and beverage . . . and a fire?

But once a year, when the dogwoods started to bloom and, paradoxically, the temperature plunged for a day or two (Dogwood Winter) Wanda gathered up her thwarted dreams and hopes and hauled them to the fire pit.

By March the fire pit, which was large enough to accommodate an ogre, had accumulated an impressive pile of leaves and pine needles and fallen limbs. To these Wanda added old tax and bank statements and candle stubs to get the fire going. Then, moving around the fire in a dance choreographed by the direction of the blustery spring wind, Wanda tossed in a year's worth of outer signs of inner pain. Photos, letters, journal pages, gifts, sensible underwear and unmatched socks all danced in the flames. The dogwood limbs leaning high above the fire pit singed but never burned. Wanda always kept a hose, as well as rage, at the ready.

Now Dogwood Winter was long gone; real winter loomed. Wanda contemplated the zigzag crack in the masonry surrounding the fireplace. She sighed audibly, solely for her own benefit since no one else was home.

Wanda's belief in cause and effect paralleled her faith in things seen and unseen; she had unswerving faith in her belief that a raging fire, the kind Thomas Wolfe's father favored in *Look Homeward,*

Angel and her husband favored in their living room, was responsible for the crack.

The doorbell rang. Wanda ushered in the chimney sweeps. They leaned down to put protective plastic covers over their shoes before spreading tarps and runners around the living room. Then they plugged their ears with protectors and turned on their massive vacuum cleaner.

Wanda went outside. She wandered down to the fire pit. Weeds flourished everywhere. Frost was still a month away. Then the dreary months of winter.

After she handed a check to the more voluble sweep, Wanda asked about the crack in the masonry. "Was it caused by a too-hot fire?" she inquired. "My fires burn all day when I start them in the morning," she added, "but my husband really piles on the logs at night."

The less voluble sweep responded, "If you want to avoid creosote build-up and a chimney fire, you need some serious heat."

"Settling caused the crack," the more voluble sweep added. "Houses settle with age and weather, and they crack. Slow burning fires are a real problem," he added. "Yes, they are. That's where you get a chimney fire."

As soon as they left, Wanda put the invoice in the back of her closet in a paper grocery bag labeled *Dogwood Winter Fire.*

CALENDARS

WHEN WANDA WAS A SCHOOL girl living at home, her father, an English teacher, whose dreams, if any, were hidden from his growing family, was unwavering in his routine of remuneration for excellence. Each of his children received a nickel for an A at report card time.

All those nickels taught Wanda the value of hard work. She felt guilty each year when she used a paid personal day to visit the City on her birthday, leaving her third graders under the questionable supervision of a substitute teacher.

Wanda never checked her luggage. She arrived at her regional airport with a small rolling suitcase and a large handbag. The handbag carried Wanda's toiletries, a spare pair of her prescription glasses, and the paperback novel she planned to read during her visit. On the return flight, two calendars replaced the novel which she finished on her third and final sleepless night in a small, noisy hotel.

Wanda passed the time during the flight home with the airline magazine. She traveled with a mechanical pencil in her handbag and was happy when no preceding passenger had attempted the Sudoku puzzle.

Wanda always journeyed up Fifth Avenue to ascend the steps of St. Patrick's Cathedral. Inside, grace and redemption were offered by unchanging installations of stained glass and altars and the vaulting, dim space.

Wanda scrabbled in the bottom of her handbag for loose change to pay for a votive candle. She appreciated the straightforward transaction. The clink of coins in the metal offering box had the solid ring of exchange and purchase. Two dollars bought you and your dearly departed a modest amount of illumination, about enough to last through dinner with espresso at the end, no dessert, and a bottle of wine shared by two drinkers who weren't slowed down by too much talk.

Some years Wanda paid for one just votive candle to illuminate more than one person, her mother and uncle, for instance. Even though they didn't seem to get along all that well while alive, she figured they'd had time to work things out and wouldn't mind sharing; or if they did, maybe being forced to share Wanda's modest contribution to their ultimate sanctification would, in and of itself, hasten the process. Besides, there never seemed to be more than two dollars change in the bottom of the handbag.

Wanda never cheated the votive candle offering box. In her moral imagination, a hidden camera ran continuous footage on some huge, heavenly monitor that displayed all sins of commission and omission and thoughts and impulses and genetic tics until the final bang when time stopped. Then each life was flash frozen, and some spiritual scanner tallied the totals, while bodies and souls, all cleverly reunited with, hopefully, varicose veins and birth defects airbrushed away, meandered to eternal bliss or torment.

Although Wanda didn't really believe in this scenario, it was, uncomfortably, no less plausible than a lot of what she did believe, or at least experience, while teaching school and raising children and waking up in her own head each morning. She would not be surprised to find that the afterlife, if there was one, was much like the paint-by-numbers pictures hung on the walls of her spiritual imagination by the humorless nuns and priests of her childhood.

Once Wanda, having four deaths in one calendar year to deal with, folded eight dollar bills until they were small enough to fit through the slot in the metal box and shoved them in. No reassuring clatter of coins emerged from the box, assuring her that her offering was acceptable. So Wanda had to ransack the bottom of her handbag for loose change and settle for just one small votive candle.

The squandering of those dollar bills still rankled.

Each year, after exiting the Cathedral, Wanda continued up Fifth Avenue to purchase two calendars at the Metropolitan Museum of Art.

Wanda felt disdain for visitors grateful for merchandise linked to a flash-in-the-pan museum experience explicated through wall introductions or, for those hiding under headphones, bossy monologues directing eyes and mind and imagination along authorized paths of experience. She inwardly mocked impulse purchases—a mug or umbrella or over-sized book—that, especially if bulky, provided an excuse to escape the challenging maze of galleries outside the exhibit. No matter what blockbuster exhibit had currently emerged from the labyrinthian process of funding and cajoling and curating, Wanda saved herself and her wallet for the main museum store.

Before her annual visit, Wanda devoutly perused the Museum catalogue that appeared in her rural delivery mailbox, imagining herself in earrings based on Roman coins in the Museum's collection or flowing scarves evocative of Tiffany windows; each year the calendars remained her only purchases.

One year a calendar's Medieval women traveled with Wanda through dentist appointments and birthdays and her daughter's first bra. Another year it was quilts that lent a splash of color to a succession of winter weeks with nothing written next to any day that in any way pertained to something Wanda wanted to do or had chosen for herself.

This year Wanda selected a year of Annunciations and left with just one calendar.

Wanda knew her father was dead. She had been to his funeral and believed her brother when he said her father was in the gray coffin she had efficiently ordered from a catalogue, while her third graders were in Physical Education, one week before his long-anticipated departure. And a candle was burning for him in St. Patrick's Cathedral. But Wanda hadn't taken in, until this moment, that this year she would be buying just one calendar.

Each year Wanda poured all her filial piety into her father's calendar. After interminable indecision and the disappointment of once again settling for Ansel Adams or the Sierra Club in the Museum store, she flew home and recorded each of his children's birthdays, wrapped the calendar in paper that could evoke either his December birthday or Christmas festivities, or both, and posted the package in plenty of time. He could open it on his birthday or wait for Christmas. Wanda was not a controlling daughter.

In exchange her father responded to her annual overture with an autumnal birthday card, never so much as a day late, signed with the tortured penmanship of a natural lefty whose childish knuckles were rapped until he submitted to the orthodoxy of the right.

Wanda experienced her growing value, as she aged, in the dollar added each year to the amount written on the check enclosed in the card from her father. Now she would just get old.

As she exited the Museum, with the shopping bag too light in her hand, the expanse of steps felt steep and uneven. A cold wind chilled foreign nannies wheeling their irritable charges out of Central Park and whipped expensive haircuts into the eyes and mouths of overburdened shoppers. Wanda hired a cab.

Safely past St. Patrick's, Wanda took the solitary calendar from its red shopping bag and removed the shrink wrap. As she turned the pages, Wanda examined each of the succession of Virgins who, waiting for her in the Museum store, insisted on being her companions this year. Some looked scared. One looked haughty. A few were very beautiful. Some were quite plain. While one or two, like the one on the cover, returned Wanda's gaze, most were looking instead at an angel and considering the angel's message.

Wanda returned the calendar to the shopping bag and rummaged in her purse for the fare. Was there an annunciation this year for her?

Wanda stepped out of the cab and walked into the restaurant. Her son was sitting at a table by the window. Wanda noted, with satisfaction, that he had already ordered their bottle of wine.

"You look great, Mom," her son beamed at her.

"That's because I'm pregnant with possibilities."

Wanda and her son clinked glasses and, fortified by their first sip of Chianti, began a serious perusal of the menu's varied offerings.

"Let's celebrate by having dessert with our espresso," Wanda suggested.

Her son looked up from the menu and returned her smile.

CHEF'S KNIFE

HE RETURNED WITHOUT HIS KNIFE, the long, lethal blade used for chopping vegetables and kept at the back of a utensil drawer behind the wooden tray Wanda's grandfather built in the damp, dark basement workshop that was Wanda's childhood refuge.

The knife traveled through Wanda's life like an autonomous element in a surreal painting. It had no agency, just presence, except for chopping vegetables.

Though once Wanda's daughter accused Wanda of attempting murder as the blade gesticulated a trenchant point during an argument in the kitchen.

When her husband left, he didn't take photos, his father's tux, or his favorite chair. He wanted to leave his dog behind too, with the vague assurance that he'd be back to fetch her someday.

Wanda demurred. She required a clean cut that might, with time, heal.

He returned without the dog or the knife. The knife was forgotten during his hasty departure, when he was banished for once again losing his traction on the slippery slope of human decency and conventions. The dog died en route.

Wanda's husband purchased a new knife with a shorter blade and a beautiful rosewood handle. Wanda's imagination quivered in disappointment.

He stored the pretty, short-bladed knife with the serrated bread knife. Wanda felt safe and sorry.

CHRISTMAS

WANDA READ THE SHOPPING LISTS out loud. The dog eyed her anxiously.

Christmas Eve

Jumbo box of pasta
Canned tomatoes
Canned tomato paste
Italian sausage
Parmesan cheese
Lettuce, peppers, cucumber, carrots
Onions and garlic
Olive oil and vinegar
Yeast and bread flour
Butter
Christmas cookie sprinkles
Molasses for gingerbread men
Jug of Gallo red wine
Ginger ale for teetotalers, including children

Christmas Morning Breakfast

Bacon
Eggs

English muffins
Strawberry jam
Granola
Yogurt
6 Grapefruits
Coffee
Half & Half

Christmas Dinner

Fearsome chunk of bloody beef
Eggplant for vegetarians
Frozen peas
Box of dehydrated mashed potatoes, like Mom made
Large, sullen rutabaga
Jar of onions for creaming
Mince pie
Pumpkin pie
Ice cream
Whipping cream
Jug of Gallo red wine
Ballantine Ale for Dad
Cider for teetotalers, including children

Next the beds. Wanda and the dog walked down the dormitory corridor, emptying the laundry basket of its borrowed sheets as they went.

The headmaster of this coed boarding school of privilege and entitlement insisted that Wanda honor the sanctity of the students' possessions if she used their rooms over the holidays. So, in addition to making up the bunks with sheets borrowed from faculty members with young children who slept in single beds, Wanda had to first strip each bunk bed and fold the sheets and put them in a closet or a drawer lest they be despoiled by Wanda's family. But Wanda quietly, secretly, drew the line at blankets and quilts. The headmaster, being a man, didn't peruse the details of these domestic arrangements too finely. He believed himself both painstaking in his obligations to the paying customers and magnanimous to his underpaid, recently bereaved staff member.

Grandfather got his own bunk in his own room, the room closest to the communal bathroom. Two brothers shared the next room and, probably, would fight over who got the top bunk. Wanda's sister and brother-in-law shared a room across the corridor from Grandfather. Her nephews got the next-door room.

Seven bottom sheets in place, Wanda returned to her apartment for top sheets and pillowcases. She stopped, dead in her tracks, bemused. The dog plowed into the back of her knees nearly toppling her. Her father. She forgot her father.

Linens for Dad. Well, her student dorm assistant owed her a favor. After all, Wanda didn't bust her when she caught a boy in her bed. Dad could sleep between the dorm assistant's high- count cotton sheets, just like Jimmy, but without the dorm assistant's company.

Wanda discovered herself sitting on the edge of the dorm assistant's bunk with her face in her hands and her eyes and nose streaming. "None of that," she muttered, wiping her face on the sleeve of her sweat shirt. The dog lay his head on her thigh. "None of that," she told him, scratching behind his ears.

By the time Wanda's sister's family arrived, delayed by a flat tire, it was 10 PM on Christmas Eve. Wanda's grandfather was just finishing his third bourbon on the rocks.

Wanda ushered, herded, cattle-prodded the family to the table, set many hours before with polished silver and top-of-the line red paper dinner napkins. (Paper napkins tonight was Wanda's only concession to herself as overwhelmed hostess of this first Christmas post-Mom; they'd have linen napkins tomorrow.) The pasta sauce was thick and rich. The salad and bread as garlicky as Mom's. The festive Gallo red as undrinkable. (Wanda's mother only served wine when she made pasta, and the wine was always Gallo red.) Wanda allowed herself to relax into eating.

After dinner, Wanda's older nephew, who had attained a semblance of literacy, read the obligatory *'Twas the Night before Christmas* while Wanda's grandfather snored quietly in his chair. Then Wanda, with forced glee, announced that it was time to hang stockings on the hooks arrayed along the bookcase.

"We'll leave the door unlocked for Santa," she assured the children. "I put a note with the cookies by the door explaining that we don't have a chimney this year."

"Did you remember a carrot for the reindeer? "Wanda's son asked.

"Go check," Wanda suggested.

"I forgot the stockings," Wanda's sister whispered.

Thin-lipped, Wanda rose and stomped to the marital bedroom. She pulled a pair of socks from her husband's drawer. He'd mind. He might even yell.

Good, she thought.

After the children and Wanda's grandfather were tucked into their beds and bunks, husbands and brothers, and Dad, settled around the tree with various beverages in hand.

"Let's do the Santa presents in the stockings and under the tree thing," Wanda said to her sister.

Wanda's sister looked stricken. "I forgot the stocking stuffers," she said. "They're still in my closet. The presents are too."

Wanda collapsed on the rug. Her sister lowered herself—she was pregnant again—beside Wanda. They hugged each other and cried.

Slowly a Christmas narrative formed in Wanda's mind. Leaving her sister in a heap, Wanda tiptoed to the desk in her bedroom and pulled a piece of paper and a pen from the drawer. Using her left hand to disguise the penmanship, Wanda wrote:

Dear Children,
My reindeer and I are so tired that we must return to the
North Pole without delivering any more presents tonight.
Wanda drew a sleepy Santa.
We'll return with your presents as soon as we rest up.
She drew a calendar with December 27, the date her sister would return to her own home, circled in red.
Thank you for your patience. Never stop believing!

Love,
S. Claus

Wanda returned to the heap that was her sister and shook it gently. Her sister pulled herself to a sitting position. Wanda handed her the note. Her sister read and smiled. Together they went out to the corridor and tucked the note under the plate with the cookies and carrot. Wanda and her sister took turns taking bites out of the carrot and cookies.

Leaving the remnants for the children to discover, they tiptoed to the closet where Wanda had hidden her children's stocking stuffers. Wanda handed her sister the bag of tangerines. Her sister put a tangerine in the toes of Wanda's children's stockings and the toes of Wanda's husband's socks. Wanda opened the two boxes of crayons and the two boxes of markers for her children and divided them into four piles. She pulled the two pads of drawing paper into four pads. She wouldn't share the bags of marbles and the kazoo and harmonica with her sister's children.

Wanda's sister wrapped the ravaged stocking stuffers in festive paper. Wanda tied ribbon around the presents, lots of ribbon. Wanda's sister propped up the packages in each stocking and sock. Wanda arranged candy canes so they stuck out enticingly.

The children's stockings and socks looked skinny and woebegone. Wanda and her sister cried a little more. Then they found their coats and hats and mittens and went out into the star-bedazzled night to link arms and sing to their mother.

COTTON FLANNEL

THE PHONE ON HER BEDSIDE table was ringing. The man beside her was snoring. A rich, slightly sweet smell of undigested scotch and overheated bodies filled her with languor and disgust. She nudged the man. He turned up the volume of his snoring.

The phone gave up. Wanda inched out of bed. Her flannel nightgown was in a heap on the floor. She picked it up, shook it briskly, and pulled it over her head. The sleeves seemed insurmountable, one inside in, the other inside out. She sat on the edge of the bed, removed the nightgown, and turned the inside out sleeve right side in. Still seated, she once again pulled the nightgown over her head then stood up slowly and let the hem find its way toward the floor.

"Want some waffles?" asked the man.

"Anything," Wanda answered. "I'll make coffee."

"When does Molly get home?"

"I have no idea. My head hurts."

"Coffee."

Muscle memory made the coffee, and Wanda sat down to the impersonal woes of the Sunday paper.

"Where *is* Molly?" her husband inquired as he scooped flour from the canister.

"Use the sifter," Wanda answered, trying to buy herself some time. (Where *was* Molly? Did she have any idea?) "I can't deal with a mouthful of baking powder this morning."

Wanda's husband dumped the flour into the eggs and milk and reached for the baking powder.

Was he being passive aggressive, Wanda wondered, or just callously indifferent?

The smell of coffee revived her.

"Molly is sleeping over at Laura's."

"How is she getting home?" her husband asked.

"In her car, I would imagine," Wanda replied with unpleasant sarcasm.

"Her car's here."

Tapping into her shallow reservoir of maternal concern, Wanda put down the paper and walked slowly and carefully into the living room. Through the window she could see Molly's car parked at a characteristically improbable angle with the seatbelt hanging out the driver's side door.

"Should I call Laura?" Wanda asked. "Do you think she's all right? What if something happened to her? Maybe the police called and I slept through it."

"Maybe she's here," her husband replied.

"What?" Wanda watched as her husband poured batter into the waffle iron.

"Maybe she's upstairs in her bed."

"Oh, shall I go look?"

"That would be one way to find out. Are you ready for a waffle?"

"Only if it's cooked enough."

"It should be ready as soon as you get back from seeing if Molly is here."

"If she's not here, I won't be hungry."

"Go."

Wanda, weighed down by parental concern and her hangover, climbed slowly up the stairs. She knocked tentatively on Molly's door.

"Molly?"

Silence. Opening the door a couple of centimeters, Wanda felt her eyes wander queasily over undulating piles of sweaters, books, shoes, candy wrappers, and soda cans. Her eyes moved anxiously to the bed. Like the floor, the bed was mounded high by a variety of objects, one of which could be Molly. Wanda opened the door just wide enough to sidle in. Lifting the hem of her nightgown, Wanda picked her way to Molly's bed. She leaned down to more closely examine the topography.

"Phew! You smell like a distillery, Mom."

Relief and the sharp throbbing of her headache reached Wanda's consciousness at the same instant.

"Your dad's making waffles. Want some?"

Molly propped herself on one elbow. "Tough night, huh? You should steer clear of Dad's buddies and stick with your herbal tea pals."

The emerald green silk of Molly's slinky nightgown contrasted nicely with her long, auburn hair. Wanda touched the hem of the sleeve.

"Where did you get this?"

"A place called Victoria's Secret, Mom. You find it by entering a mall. Victoria's Secret is where women buy things so they can feel feminine and look as if they were born in this century."

"Well, just don't wear it outside this room!"

"Right, Mom." Molly slipped under the covers.

"Your waffle's getting cold," Wanda heard her husband call up the stairs.

"I'll be down in a minute."

Wanda went into the bathroom, splashed cold water on her face, and brushed her teeth and hair. Head held high, she marched down the stairs and into the kitchen.

Her husband looked up from the paper and his waffle. "Was Molly there?"

"Alas, yes."

"Is that a new nightgown?"

"Yeah, you got it from L.L.Bean's for my birthday."

"I like it on you. Flannel's sexy. It leaves a lot to the imagination."

Wanda's husband took a big mouthful of syrupy waffle. Wanda sat down. She picked up the paper then set it down again.

"You know, I really love you," she said.

Through a muffle of waffle and syrup, Wanda was sure she heard, "I really love you too."

DEADHEADING DAYLILIES

WANDA DEFINED EACH DAY, IN June and July, by deadheading daylilies.

During her children's childhood, she woke before them and went, crusty-eyed and barefoot, into the dewy morning, with a basket or bag, to gather the wasted flowers for the compost pile. When she was feeling hopeful and fond of her life and its occupants, deadheading the day lilies was a chance to notice the new flowers that appeared (as miraculously as fireflies in the evening) morning after morning until, finally, there were no more buds and the August heat of a Southern summer had arrived.

After her children were grown, Wanda had a decade of desperation. Her new garden was urban and full of mosquitoes and ticks. Her mornings had the taste of nicotine and caffeine and despair. Each evening in June and July, before the fireflies, Wanda would sever each daylily flower (innocently blooming, in ignorance of its imminent mortality) with a kitchen knife. She'd arrange a pattern, a prayer rug of blooms, on a tray, in bowls, on a table. She'd frantically take in their intricate beauty during the hours before bedtime—a ruffled petal, a crimson center, a delicate scent. The next morning, while the coffee dripped, she'd clean up the sodden mess, wipe up the stains, especially purple, and carry the carnage through still-damp grass to the compost pile. She'd block the day's new flowers from her eyes and heart until that evening, before the fireflies, when she could harvest and hoard and mourn them.

When finally a grandmother, Wanda woke each morning with the excitement she felt, long ago, on Christmas mornings and Easter mornings, when magic happened while she slept. While the sky brightened, she drank coffee. Then, In June and July, barefoot and alert, she wandered her rural yard, rife with ticks and moles and squirrels, to deadhead the spent daylilies and celebrate each new bloom.

DODGING DUTY

WANDA SANK INTO THE SYBARITIC beach chaise lounge and accepted a beaded glass of tonic and lime from Kevin, who was a shorter, more accessible version of Michelangelo's David. The sky was blue. The sun was yellow/white. Waves crashed. Children scuttered like crabs close to the shore.

Selfishness cocooned Wanda in the shade of her meticulously angled beach umbrella; it was situated by a thuggish employee of the beach paraphernalia franchise which had, Wanda felt certain, ties to the Florida Mafia.

SPF 50 sunscreen, applied in her room before actual exposure to the sun's deadly rays, should forestall a visit to Wanda's dermatologist who, regrettably, recently chopped short her dramatic wiry hair and plucked her unruly eyebrows. While Wanda didn't fault anyone's accommodation to the onslaught of age, she did regret her dermatologist's accompanying loss of a buoyant cheerfulness that cushioned all the freezing and scraping of Wanda's sun- and age-ravaged face.

Wanda took a long sip of her tonic and put the glass back in the chaise lounge's cup holder. She removed her straw hat and her terry cloth cover all and rose, as gracefully as she could, from her chair.

Wanda walked past an oversized beach towel with its undersized Brazilian bikini. Her walk became a jog as she noticed a pair of unruly boys—brothers? she wondered—who reminded her of the grandsons she didn't bring to the beach. Wanda ran into the ocean and dove headlong into the waves.

Wanda caught three good waves, the last one so powerful that it filled her suit with sand as she body surfed all the way to the shore. She waded out deep enough to empty sand from the crotch of her suit and slick back her hair. Then she sauntered to her South Beach real estate and signaled to the deeply tanned and muscled Kevin.

"I'd like a gin and tonic now, please," Wanda said. "It's five o'clock somewhere."

DRAGON DREAM

Hello, Hello.
Let me tell you what it's like to be a zero, zero.
Let me show you what it's like to never feel, feel.
Like I'm good enough for anything that's real, real.
I'm looking for a way out . . .

"I KIND OF LIKE THAT song," Wanda said.

Her granddaughter glanced over from the Disney movie credits.

"Well, you'll like the name of the band too."

"What is it?"

"Imagine Dragons."

"Really?"

"Really."

"Do you like them?" Wanda asked.

"Not really," her granddaughter answered. "I don't like boy bands."

"Right, said Wanda. "Time for bed."

Wanda didn't have to turn on the light and glance at the clock on her bedside table. She knew it was 3 AM. The Hour of the Wolf. Or, in this case, the Hour of the Dragon.

Something always woke her halfway through the night. She usually wasn't sure what it was: A heavy meal? An extra glass of red wine? Regret? But this night it was most certainly a dragon.

Wanda had always assumed that dragons were male. But that

made no sense. There had to be female dragons or how could dragons continue to propagate and occupy their niche in the human imagination?

Wanda's dragon was in a dark cave with an enormous rock covering the entrance, a rock so huge and heavy that only the tiniest sliver of light could enter through a small crack at the top.

The cave had a funky smell that Wanda found unpleasant. It smelled of clothes that needed washing, not from sweaty exercise but from being worn again and again, without purpose or joy. The dragon herself had the used-up smell of an un-lived life, a smell that reminded Wanda of her seventh-grade math teacher, who kept a tissue tucked in the sleeve of her dress. The bottom of the teacher's arm jiggled when she retrieved the tissue, and her body odor wafted through the air.

Wanda's dream contained the dragon's dream. Her dragon dreamed of dragon eggs, three eggs, perfect translucent spheres. Her dragon tossed and moaned, scales worn thin, waiting to be rescued, dreaming of her eggs. One egg contained a unicorn. One a fair maiden. The third contained St. George, slayer of dragons.

Wanda pulled herself out of her tumbled and tossed blankets and sheets and stumbled to the kitchen, groping in the dark for tea kettle and mug and tea bag. She waited for the water to roil like some ancient, angry sea, poured it into her mug, and returned to her bed.

While she sipped the tea, propped up in her bed by pillows rescued from the floor, she decided that tomorrow—today, actually—she'd wash the sheets and air the house and move through the hours recorded in her calendar as things to do and hours that had no shape, not yet.

She'd bake cookies with her granddaughter.

DRY CREEK

WANDA MEASURED OUT ESPRESSO, SCREWED on the top of the espresso pot, and turned up the flame on the stove. Her lassitude was alarming. The Vernal Equinox had come and gone, the day was turning beautiful, she could do whatever she wanted, at home or out in the world. So why was she lolling about like a gangly teenager who was growing so fast that there was no energy for anything else.

Wanda was not growing. If anything, she was shrinking. Fortunately, Wanda had a tacit agreement with the nurse who weighed and measured her at her annual physical. As long as her heels remained on the floor, Wanda could take as much time as required to stretch her torso until her height achieved sixty-two inches. Each year it took a little longer.

Wanda attributed her current torpor and moodiness to a "Spring Is Here" malaise. No desire, no ambition moved her. Nobody loved her best of all, and, she had to admit to herself, she felt old and broken and, also, a little guilty. Of what?

Wanda hung a load of laundry on the line. She imagined the sunshine she'd smell in her napkin and pillows that evening. She took a bucket of scraps out to the composter. And at last the espresso—bitter, black, and potent—was ready!

Wanda sat in the sun sipping slowly and deliberately, not at all like an Italian woman, her gorgeous calves toned from all that walking up steep cobblestoned streets, standing at the bar just long enough for a quick shot of espresso before she swished elegantly and purposefully out the door.

Wanda was practicing mindfulness.

And procrastinating.

Wanda's least favorite spring task was cleaning out the dry creek.

"Don't do it," her husband exhorted each March. He didn't worry that the rocks, so artfully arranged in a long, shallow, narrow ditch that paralleled the house and sloped down to the flood plain, would disappear under composting pine needles and leaves. Wanda was the worrier.

Wanda wondered, as she did each March, why, instead of a creative, beautiful dry creek, there wasn't a pedestrian, buried drain pipe. Even after a torrential rainstorm, the dry creek never functioned as it should. Something about it—the pitch or the size and shape of the rocks or the paradoxical name—just wasn't quite right.

What were they thinking? Wanda wondered, as she rinsed the mug and the espresso pot.

Wanda was wary of ticks and copperheads. She wished, as she did every March, that she had undertaken the leaf-blowing and raking and hand-removing of leaves and needles and twigs in late winter.

But, as was the case every February, she preferred to sit by the fire. Branches of yellow forsythia and white winter honeysuckle brightened and perfumed the room as Wanda waited for spring. Then she and the ticks and copperheads emerged.

Halfway down the dry creek, after she hauled three large plastic baskets of needles and leaves and twigs to the other side of the house and spread them under the blackberry bushes, Wanda realized there was no beer in the fridge. No beer to savor in the late afternoon sun as she sat by the pond imagining ticks settling into her body's crevices and scalp. No beer to sip as she watched the goldfish dart around the pond, having escaped, so far, the attention of the Blue Heron who had eaten all their predecessors. No beer to make her nostalgic for the beer o'clock tradition, after working on whatever property she and her husband currently called home, as the sun set and sweat grew clammy on their skin.

Just as well, Wanda told herself, quite sternly.

DYING OF THIRST

"My pretty little girl." Wanda's mother touched her gently on the forehead and continued down the stairs.

Wanda's eyes stung, but she didn't cry.

The other time her mother told her she was pretty Wanda was fifteen and ready for a school dance. Her mother had sounded surprised that her dull, homely Wanda had done something so unexpected.

Wanda's mother reached the bottom of the stairs and pivoted to enter the living room. Wanda followed.

Her mother circled the room touching a hunting print, her desk, the dry sink converted to a bar. Then she went to the kitchen. She took a silver teaspoon from the dish drainer and scooped droplets of water from the bottom of the sink. Wanda listened to the clinking of the spoon as it tapped against the porcelain.

When the surgeon said her mother was dying of cancer and required breast surgery, Wanda's mother asked him what he planned to do with do with her breast. Wanda looked at her mother. Her mother started to laugh. Wanda began laughing too. By the time they finished suggesting places and uses for the soon-to-be amputated breast, tears were streaming down both of their faces.

The surgeon left the examination room.

The sound of the spoon scraping porcelain stopped. Wanda's mother turned on both taps and rinsed the spoon. Then she put the teaspoon back in the dish drainer and entered the sun room. She stood by the bay window where impatiens and begonias bloomed between small round rocks she had once gathered from a mountain stream. Wanda watched as her mother moved the rocks according to some inscrutable pattern. Then her mother picked up the mister and began spraying her plants.

Wanda's mother put down the mister and looked confused. Wanda led her to the sofa. She read Annie Dillon to her mother. Her mother had started the book with her book group in the before times.

Wanda's reading was interrupted by her father's arrival home for lunch.

Her father was a man of habits. He did his morning push-ups, took his midday nap after lunch, drank a martini before dinner, and lay down beside his wife each night. He set the thermostat to sixty degrees when the furnace was turned on in late fall. He kept it at sixty degrees until spring.

Wanda turned up the thermostat during the day. (Her mother was always cold.) Her father turned down the thermostat when he got home from work, before he changed into khakis and fixed his martini.

Wanda never discussed the details of dying with her father.

EYE OF THE DRAGON

WANDA SAT IN A COFFEE shop attached to the faux Gothic university library, contentedly sipping a small latte with an extra shot of espresso. Her brother was out of her sight lines, but she imagined him happily bowed over a tome containing arcane family history, a tome only available far away from his home and close to Wanda's.

Abstruse details found no hook in Wanda's memory closet. Just what her brother was hoping to discover had joined the heap on the closet floor.

What she would never forget, however, was the ethereal being who handed the book to her brother.

"The book," the angelic apparition whispered, "the book should probably stay in the library because it's so very precious and rare. It's my job to mention that rule," she softly apologized.

Wanda's brother retreated to a carrel with his rare book, blinking in glorious, golden wonder.

The vision admonished Wanda, "Please take him outside soon to the sunshine and gardens."

In answer to Wanda's question, she pointed a slender, translucent finger in the direction of the coffee shop.

Outside the coffee shop was a kiosk of bins filled with periodicals. Wanda sighed her delight. To peruse newsprint and consume caffeine at the same time was a quaint and atavistic experience seldom achieved anymore.

She settled at a table by a window that looked out on a terrace powdered with yellow pollen.

Dominating the top half of the front page was a black circle with a glowing nimbus. The caption claimed that she was looking at a photograph of a black hole.

Wanda's "Oh no!" was sufficiently audible to turn heads in her direction. She felt her eyes fill with tears and her cheeks turn hot.

A black hole was supposed to be hypothetical, Einstein's worst nightmare, and Hawkins', where laws and logic and methodology and belief were pressed and compressed until what? Darkness consumed all light?

After sitting, stunned, and sipping for a while, Wanda read the article. A young woman's algorithm guided them, the people all over the globe, as they photographed and collated image after image, never talking or whispering or tweeting to each other what they saw, never tweaking what they were seeing to fit a grand hypothesis. And then the final image, the dance of all those photos, became the nightmare come true, the glowing eye of the dragon, dark at dead-center and bottomless, the glowing abyss.

Still, Wanda told herself in a prosaic inner voice, it's a gazillion miles away in a different galaxy.

But today it was on the front page of the paper that had been by her father's cereal bowl each morning for as long as she could remember, a real paper, not a tabloid. It had travelled all those gazillion miles on its journey to all those telescopes that merged their images into what she was looking at, recoiling from.

Wanda ripped the image from the paper—heads turned again—and folded it and put it in her bag. She found her brother waiting for her by the desk, the golden apparition replaced by a dingy graduate student, and together they wandered gardens showered with pollen.

Eyes watering and throat clogged, Wanda considered the abyss ringed with light. We may never need to know what happens inside, she decided.

FUNDAMENTALLY
SERIOUS DISPOSITION

ONE FEBRUARY AFTERNOON WANDA UNDERTOOK the file cabinet in her studio.

While not a hoarder, Wanda was a saver. Or, perhaps, a discerning hoarder of objects with personal significance, such as

hair cut from her horse's mane before he was given away
motel paper inscribed with *Molly heart Mom*
African stamps from a missionary friend
a file labeled *Recommendations*

Wanda opened the file. The first letter was written by a former, older friend, an excellent teacher at a mediocre boarding school, who always seemed, to Wanda, more plausible as an impecunious but learned country clergyman. Her friend, with his bossy wife and churlish students, was quietly, politely, desperately miserable. Like Wanda's horse, her friend died of sorrow.

Wanda read the recommendation he wrote at her request. It was succinct and precise and had been helpful in getting her a teaching job at a slightly less mediocre day school. But It didn't describe Wanda as she wanted to be seen—funny and cheerful and whimsical. Wanda's suicidal colleague saw a different Wanda and permanently pinned her, or so she felt, to a specimen board.

He said, "The applicant is of a fundamentally serious disposition."

Because of that sentence, Wanda could never lightly skim the surface of life, like dragonflies dancing on the surface of a lake or the tiny blue butterflies that hovered over the manure pile behind the barn. She was a plodder, heavy-footed, level-headed, with a furrow deepening between her brows.

Wanda slid the life sentence back into the manila folder, closed the file cabinet drawer, and returned to her kitchen for a sensible cup of tea.

GINGERBREAD MEN

WANDA GLARED UP AT THE green box. It huddled forlornly in the far corner of the cupboard above the stove, partly hidden by a bag of flour. She hoisted herself up onto the counter beside the stove and contorted her upper body around the open cupboard door. She shoved the bag of flour to the back of the cupboard and groped blindly for the box. Index cards flew like giant snowflakes as the box bounced off the counter and fell to the floor. Wanda counted to ten very slowly. She would not swear at her mother's recipe box on Christmas Eve.

"Come look at the lights on the tree," a cheerful voice called from the living room.

"Come look at the recipe cards on the floor," Wanda called back.

Wanda felt a pang. Her husband was proud of the five strings of blinking lights he bought for the tree this year. It was Christmas Eve. She should go look at the tree.

But she didn't want to go look at five hundred epilepsy-inducing blinking lights that her husband would insist they turn on tonight and every other night until the Twelfth Day of Christmas when the Three Wise Men finally made it to Bethlehem and she could strip the tree, vacuum the needles, throw out the fruitcake, and wait for spring.

Wanda stayed in the kitchen and shuffled through the index cards strewn on the kitchen floor.

Chicken cacciatore. Artichoke Dip. Zucchini Frittata.

"Where the hell are Mom's damned gingerbread men," she muttered.

Meat Loaf Surprise. Tuna Casserole. Chocolate Mousse.

The Gingerbread Men card smelled faintly of ginger and cinnamon.

Wanda took a stick of butter from the fridge. She opened the cupboard next to the fridge and found the jar of molasses. She pulled down the bag of sugar from the cupboard over the stove, bumping her head on the open door, and dropped the bag of sugar on the counter.

"Shit!"

"Wanda," called a disapproving voice from the living room.

Wanda reached into the cupboard by the stove for a saucepan. She reached into the cupboard above the stove for a measuring cup.

Boil 1/2 c molasses.

Wanda did.

Add 1/4 c sugar.

The measuring cup was sticky with molasses. Wanda shrugged and measured 1/4 c of sugar. She managed to scrape most of it into the saucepan with a spoon.

1 T milk

Wanda sighed. She walked slowly back to the refrigerator. She carried the half gallon of milk to the stove. The measuring spoons hung on their hook next to the refrigerator. Wanda sighed again. She trudged back across the kitchen for the spoons and back to the stove for the milk and carried them over to the sink. She held the tablespoon over the sink and splashed milk into it. With her spare hand cupped under the brimming tablespoon, she shuffled slowly back to the stove.

Sift 2 c flour, 1/2 tsp baking soda, salt, nutmeg, cinnamon, powdered cloves, and 1 tsp ginger.

The bag of flour clung to the back of the cupboard beyond Wanda's reach. She pulled herself up on the counter again and blindly pulled the bag toward her, willing it to stay upright. It did.

The sifter was on the top shelf of the cupboard behind the cheese grater. Wanda straightened up as much as she could, while staying on her knees, and felt for the sifter. She set it on the counter next to the flour and lowered herself back down to the floor.

Wanda filled the sifter to the two-cup mark.

The baking soda and salt perched cooperatively within reach on the front of the bottom shelf above the stove. Wanda measured them into the sifter.

Wanda squared her shoulders and marched over to the spice rack. It hung by itself, far from the debilitating heat of the stove. Each identical jar displayed Wanda's labels.

"Allspice, basil, caraway seeds, chili powder, cinnamon, cloves, coriander, cream of tartar, cumin, curry powder, dill weed, fennel, ginger, mustard, mustard seed, nutmeg, paprika, rosemary, sage, tarragon, thyme," Wanda murmured to herself.

Equanimity restored, Wanda unscrewed the jars and measured the spices. Then she screwed back the tops and replaced each jar in its allotted space.

Wanda lifted the sifter.

"Damn!"

She glanced nervously at the living room. Not a creature was stirring, nor reprimanding. But five hundred Christmas lights were blinking nervously.

Wanda turned back to the growing mound of white on the counter below the sifter. She set the sifter down again.

"Mohammed will come to the mountain," she muttered.

She grabbed the saucepan from the stove and set it on the

counter. Then she lifted it up quickly and spit on the index finger of her free hand. She touched the bottom of the pan. Cool enough.

Wanda sifted the dry ingredients into the saucepan and swept the dry ingredients on the counter into the saucepan too.

Add more flour if needed.

Wanda turned the card over.

Nothing. Not another word.

"Thanks, Mom," she said.

The front door slammed. The hall closet slammed.

"Wow! Awesome tree, Dad!"

Then Molly filled the kitchen. Her cheeks were as red as her hair. Molly walked over to Wanda and peered into the saucepan.

"Grannie's gingerbread, Mom? I've been so totally depressed about no gingerbread men on the tree this year. Is it her recipe?"

Wanda pointed to the card.

Molly glanced at the directions, turned over the card, and started to laugh.

"Grannie never wasted any words did she, Mom? Not like us."

Molly put a sympathetic arm around Wanda. Wanda noticed that Molly was a good two inches taller than she was. She hoped Molly was wearing platform shoes.

"When's dinner?" Molly asked.

"Ask your dad. He's cooking as soon as I vacate the kitchen."

Molly vanished.

Wanda set the oven to somewhere between 350 and 375 degrees, a compromise cookie- baking temperature.

A memory of her mother spreading flour on the counter, laying waxed paper over a mound of gingerbread, and rolling the dough popped up like an unsolicited ad. Wanda's hands mimicked the memory until the dough flattened beneath her mother's rolling pin. Then she pressed the dented gingerbread man cookie cutter into the dough.

The first three gingerbread men were amputees. But then the cookie cutter overcame Wanda's clumsiness. One for her husband. One for her son.

One for her daughter. One for herself.

"So sexist," Wanda muttered. "Patriarchal," through clenched teeth.

Wanda slid the cookie sheet into the oven.

A small mound of dough remained on the counter. Wanda picked it up and shaped it into head, torso, legs, and arms.

"Run, run as fast as you can. You can't catch me, I'm the gingerbread man," she said, on behalf of her mother.

She found her husband and dog in front of the TV. Both looked at her. She handed the dough to the dog and kissed her husband on the top of his head.

"I'm almost finished in the kitchen," she said.

GRADUATING

WANDA OPENED THE BOX. FOR three years she had known she'd be giving the pin to her daughter. But suddenly it seemed hard, or at least unsettling. Molly already had so much. The ruthlessness of youth. Astonishing beauty. A boyfriend. Knowledge of VCRs.

Wanda remembered when she received the pin. It took her awhile to figure out how long ago that had been. The result of her mental calculations was disturbing. Almost thirty years ago she was getting ready for her own high school graduation.

She wore her sister's dress. It fit, more or less, and eliminated the irksome need to shop. Her mother came into the room and handed her a small, blue box. Her mother had a strange, strained look on her face as she handed the box to Wanda. When Wanda opened the box, she saw her mother's pearl pin. She remembered thanking her mother. Maybe they hugged; she couldn't recall.

Wanda didn't like the pin. Most jewelry confused her, suggesting as it did a definite choice beyond the practical necessity of wearing clothes. But she wore the pin on her graduation dress.

Mainly the pin sat in its blue box in her bureau drawer. It was a talisman of her mother's attempt at love. Wanda looked at it from time to time. Soon, if she wanted to look at the pin, she'd have to find it in the jumble of Molly's drawers and closet. If Molly didn't lose it or give it away. She hoped Molly wouldn't.

Wanda pulled out the bureau drawer that held her boxes of old jewelry, jewelry that would always belong to her mother. When, rarely, she put on this jewelry, she saw her mother fasten a pin or necklace and brush past Wanda in a haze of perfume.

Molly had her own graduation dress. Wanda admired her for that. Molly shopped for three hours before finding the graduation dress she would wear.

"I think this is the one, Mom."

Warily, Wanda raised her eyes. Molly's eyes met hers in the mirror, imploring Wanda to affirm all that vulnerable flesh.

"You're right!" Wanda answered with forced enthusiasm.

The dress required a backless, strapless bra. Wanda hadn't known there were backless, strapless bras, but Molly knew just where to find one.

Wanda looked down at the blue box and realized Molly's graduation present wasn't good enough for Molly.

Wanda felt annoyed. The pin was, after all, both valuable and sentimental. She had been enjoying the serenity—smugness, actually—of having Molly's graduation present settled.

Wanda put the blue box in her purse. She searched for her keys. She headed for her car. Drove downtown. Parked (badly). Trudged through a spirit-numbing drizzle to the antique jewelry store.

Molly's graduation earrings were very fine and very old. Wanda would never know who wore them before, whose skin oils had given them such a valuable luster. But she did know, because her friend who owned the antique jewelry store assured her, that they went well with Molly's graduation pin. As Wanda held an earring to the pin, she caught a glimpse of an ideal, harmonious world with Molly marching bravely through it.

She wrote her friend a check and drove home through heavy rain.

Wanda took the boxes out of her purse. Her friend had wrapped them in elegant white paper and tied each with a silk ribbon, one green, one blue.

The front door slammed. Molly was home.

HAWK

WANDA WATCHED AS THE HAWK landed by the pond. She wondered if it were related to the hawk she held once, protected by a long, thick leather glove that, like the hawk, belonged to her friend. Though the word *belonged* didn't work for the hawk as well as it did for the glove. Wanda remembered the hawk's freedom quivering beneath its training.

Wanda was living alone then, like now, and felt more fearless than when family hovered and opined. Wanda liked living alone, surrounded by wild creatures and her gardens. Rabbits ate her lettuce and her balloon flowers. Moles and voles ate the roots of whatever they encountered as they heaved up the ground.

Wanda didn't mind. She could replace the vegetables and herbs and flowers at the grocery store or farmers' market. She had options; the creatures didn't.

And the deer were fenced out. Total, overnight devastation wasn't likely, just annoyance.

Wanda watched the hawk fly over the trees and disappear. It was hard to believe it could be related to the hawk that perched on her hand while her friend hovered anxiously nearby. But of course the hawks were related. Everything's related, Wanda thought.

Wanda's stomach heaved and she had to put her head between her knees. She was no longer related to her husband, or wouldn't be soon, though half-a-century of sharing a life connected them. And half-a-century of fighting for her life.

Wanda stood up. She examined her ring finger. You could hardly tell it had been banded. She wondered if the hawk she once held minded being banded around its leg with a leather strap, to prevent it from flying away.

Since her husband left, this time, finally, for good, Wanda barely registered the black snake stealing the cardinal's eggs from the nest in the Carolina Jasmine. She no longer felt like taking sides. She barely remarked the dead doe in the pond, attacked and chased by coyotes, as it sank a bit further under the surface each week. In a month she'd be swimming with the decaying doe, as well as snapping turtles and dragonflies. Wanda wondered, without much interest, if the snapping turtles were responsible for the gradual disappearance of the doe.

Each morning Wanda woke early, before dawn, to see what would happen next. She had traded the illusion of agency, in the narrative of her life, for curiosity.

HEAR, HEAR

FOR THE FIRST WEEK SHE felt insane. Her husband's voice was loud and clear, except he wasn't speaking. There were other phantom sounds. Loud construction equipment only she could hear while riding horses on a peaceful trail. A whine. A drone. Chimes. She kept waiting for the voice of her guardian angel who guided her, ineptly, through adolescence.

When the tinnitus went away, it was replaced by profound unilateral silence.

The available nurse practitioner cheerfully suggested Flonase.

When that did no good, a specialist told her the cause of her deafness would be understood when she had an autopsy and prescribed waiting six months to see, or hear, if Wanda's ear miraculously functioned again.

Wanda's neighbor brought over bone conduction headphones which, when plugged into Wanda's laptop, enabled her to hear perfectly. Jubilation.

Until Wanda realized she couldn't plug into people. Despair.

Hearing aids helped a little. But the location of the sounds they amplified was a mystery. Wanda spun like a top trying to find the bird or person she was hearing.

Wanda's husband couldn't accommodate himself to Wanda and her new world. His voice startled her until she found him; he never showed himself before he spoke.

Wanda gave up large gatherings and her marriage. She was too deaf to deal with the former and not deaf enough for the latter.

That winter Wanda sat contentedly by the fire, hearing aids in their ingenious charging case, listening to the muted background noises of her peaceful home. The heat pump's fan gently whirred. The dryer spun. The fire crackled. All so gently. No one spoke.

In the beginning was the Word. In the end will be Silence, blessed Silence, and a vast, spacious, peace.

HIVES

WANDA WOKE AT 2 AM. The itching overcame her daytime decision to forego Benadryl with its brain-cell-decimating reputation.

Groggily she turned on the bathroom light and rummaged in the drawer where she last recalled encountering the pink pills. She kept a small stash hidden in her box of Q tips.

For the last several weeks Wanda had been plagued by huge welts that appeared at the top of her neck and forehead, unsightly and intolerably itchy. Wanda researched her affliction and discovered that one of several possible autoimmune disorders would undoubtedly force her to scratch her way into oblivion.

A less dramatic website suggested hives. Stress-related hives.

Over half a century before, Wanda stood at the altar, only dimly aware of her soon-to-be husband. Wanda felt no particular connection to this slim, trim version of the man she agreed to marry a year ago. That man sported a cheerful beer belly and was missing a tooth. This serious, sober man, with his Marine Corps training and gleaming smile, seemed disciplined and dull.

Wanda experienced a near death experience. Her soul hovered above Wanda incarnate who, following the priest's directions, vowed her life away.

When the wedding pictures arrived for her perusal and selection, Wanda chose to include the picture that recorded her body's mute protest to the ritual it underwent. From cleavage to chin, the mottled bride was festooned with hives.

Wanda wondered why the photographer failed to edit that image or discreetly discard it. Wanda wondered why she included it among the pictures that immortalized the day.

Wanda lay beneath the covers waiting for the Benadryl to make her drowsy enough to sleep.

IRISH

WANDA WASN'T IRISH. SHE WAS happy to be not Irish. That country, with its wet wildness and spirit trapped in bottles of whiskey and Guinness, and its superstition and misogyny, was not Wanda's home.

It was not St. Patrick's home either. St. Patrick was captured by pirates and deposited by them on the shores of Ireland where he tidied up Irish spirituality, pagan and quirky, with the official religion of the Holy Roman Empire, post Constantine, legalistic and hierarchical. Any bits and pieces were stuffed out of sight under the blue mantle of the Virgin Mary, sexless Mother of God, and don't mess with her or your own mother if you know what's good for you.

Patrick also rid Ireland of its snake problem, drove them all away, into the depths, out of the light of day.

Wanda was deposited In Ireland with her husband, seeking his melancholy roots and his true home, on a summer vacation funded by his wee inheritance. They scrambled up the scree-covered slope of Croagh Patrick (Croagh is Irish for Mountain) passing pilgrims on their hands and knees. The pilgrims crawled from one station of the cross (twelve in all) to the next until they achieved the chapel at the summit with, Wanda hoped, a sense of accomplishment commensurate with their blood and bruises.

Wanda and her husband spent their first night in Ireland at a modest B&B with a claustrophobia of patterns and bric-a-brac and the heavy breakfast of eggs and rashers and sausage and tomatoes that was to be their morning repast for two long weeks.

After breakfast Wanda sat in the dark, fussy parlor writing in her journal. When their hostess had finished the washing up, she joined Wanda. Her calloused, reddened hands were holding a piece of fabric that looked both coarse and fragile. Wanda's hostess looked at Wanda expectantly so Wand obligingly asked, "What's that?"

"It's the caul of my first-born son," the hostess explained. "He was born with the caul about him. As long as I keep it safe, he shall not perish in the sea."

Before Wanda could compose a response, her hostess turned and left the parlor.

Soon Wanda and her husband got in their rented car and drove to the first sight their guidebook recommended, though what that was Wanda never could recall.

JIGSAW PUZZLE

Wanda felt like a jigsaw puzzle with boring but critical pieces missing. A bit of blue sky, part of the puzzle's border, or a purple-blue violet on the undifferentiated green of grass.

The world appeared, to Wanda, who was born with monocular vision, as flat as a painting on the cover of a puzzle. Like an artist, Wanda tricked her mind into imagining depth and distance.

Also missing from Wanda's world was a sense of direction. Wanda never knew whether to turn right or left to arrive at the restaurant with a blue awning and red geraniums perennially blooming in the window, even if they did look a little straggly by February.

Wanda's friends were never annoyed. Wanda, among her circle of intimates, was famously unable to remember where objects were located in space and time; from keys and wallet to blue-awning restaurant. But she never forgot a birthday or divulged a secret.

So each of her friends waited patiently, with water or wine or coffee or tea, for Wanda to rush into the restaurant with myriad excuses and apologies.

Enormous black-winged butterflies beat against Wanda's belly, attempting to exit through her navel. The butterflies were new arrivals, upsetting the ecosystem of her world. Her personal climate change. Harbingers of imminent disaster. What if, the black butterflies battered mercilessly, the time came when Wanda set out to meet someone and forgot they were meeting at the restaurant with the blue awning and brave geraniums? What if, when she got to the stoplight, it was no longer just a question of saying, "Shit!" and turning left and going two miles and saying "Shit" again and backtracking and going three miles in the other direction and being apologetically late.

To placate the god of forgetfulness and his black butterfly minions Wanda heaped blueberries on her cereal each morning, mixing science and magical thinking at the start of each day. She planted blueberry bushes in her yard and spent sweaty hours each summer at a u-pick blueberry farm. Her freezer bulged with bags of berries, individually flash-frozen on cookie sheets during hot summer days.

She solved Sudoku puzzles.

Wanda suspected it would be equally efficacious, and far less labor-intensive, to steal into some dimly lit Catholic church to light a candle and say a prayer to the omnipotent god of her childhood. But churches had become brighter, with tiers of chairs in a semi-circle around a stage where a cheerful priest, assisted by people of all ages and sexes and degrees of grooming, prepared a Happy Meal for anyone who was hungry.

JOB

WANDA FELT HER TOEHOLD SLIPPING, like the time she went rock climbing with her nephew. The line her nephew had fastened to her halter anchored her; but when her foot slipped, she felt, for a second or three, that she was in a forever free fall.

Wanda was anchored to her life by place and living things: creek, trees, birds who required that she feed them and squirrels who stole their food. The sun moved across her sky, low in the winter, high in the summer. During the winter months, trapped in the house, Wanda followed the sun like a cat. She ate and wrote and read and daydreamed at tables and in chairs, from eastern to western windows, following the warmth of the low, slanting light.

Wanda also had habits and routines to keep her safely tethered. She walked briskly through the woods, practiced yoga, ate meals full of grains and vegetables, drank measured doses of caffeine and spirits, lunched with friends, meditated with seekers.

And she used to have her husband.

Now there was no one to test the safety line or check the handholds and footholds. Wanda felt herself falling down instead of climbing up. She didn't know what she'd do when she reached the bottom. Die?

So Wanda applied for a job.

When Wanda heard the message—it startled her from a nap by the fire on a chilly Dogwood Winter day—she felt an exultant, lifting joy. She had been hired to water plants, had a place to go each afternoon, as the days lengthened and warmed. She was a real person again, small but solid, for now at least, for the months when nursery plants woke up from dormancy and seedlings put down roots.

KALEIDOSCOPE

THE POSTMAN COMETH, THOUGHT WANDA, cringing at the pedestrian word play/literary allusion humor she inherited from her father, along with his twitchiness and devotion to routine.

Still, having the mail person—they seemed to last just a month or two on her route—dare to enter the yard (Wanda now left the gate unlocked) and put packages on the porch was a brightly colored piece of her new life.

Wanda imagined her life as a kaleidoscope. She played with one as a child. It was a cheap stocking stuffer made of cardboard. Wanda contentedly turned the moveable attachment to transform the pattern of shapes and colors until it fell apart.

Later she acquired a handsome wooden kaleidoscope, a thoughtful present from her husband. When it seemed like the dark pieces dominated its patterns, she set the present aside.

And then she set aside her husband.

Wanda took a deep and bright pleasure in chopping green and purple cabbage for a slaw or hanging dish towels and sheets on the line or sweeping the kitchen floor or carpet-sweeping the living room rug. She didn't miss the darkness of her husband's unexpected rages, his noisy chainsaw and lawn mower, the vacuum cleaner banging against furniture and doors.

In time the grass began to grow and grow some more. Wanda reluctantly cranked up her husband's noisy lawn mower. She pushed it across the lawn once and returned it to the shed. She ordered a lawn mower as quiet as the carpet sweeper.

Wanda opened the long cardboard box that the mail person left on her porch. She removed the shiny chrome handles and the heavy, sharp blades. There was a diagram. Wanda slowly assembled her green and orange mower.

After lunch Wanda moved the mower from the deck and set it on the lawn next to the smooth, wide path her husband's mower had noisily cut through the grass. She pushed her mower across the lawn. It left a narrow path and a couple of dandelions in its wake.

KITCHEN CLOCK

WANDA KEPT THE KITCHEN CLOCK set to Daylight Savings Time. Her reasons were both practical and philosophical. First, the clock was high above the kitchen sink and required a stepladder to reach. Second, time was arbitrary enough without the Authorities decreeing changes twice a year.

Wanda's patience and persistence, while the outer world shifted by an hour, was rewarded, always, by the outer world returning to the time above her kitchen sink.

Wanda's sister gave her the kitchen clock many years ago when she still gave out presents on red-letter holidays and birthdays. Her presents were usually handmade by a friend or purchased at a crafts fair. Often Wanda resented the obligatory thank-you note for a misshapen basket of inscrutable purpose or a scarf with tassels so long they gathered dust and lint as they moved through Wanda's day. But Wanda loved the clock and suspected her sister loved her, as she sometimes did, when she made the purchase.

The kitchen clock ran on a single tiny battery in a holder glued to the back of the plate. Wanda couldn't recall if the battery was AA or AAA because it seemed as close to immortal as possible in this earthly realm; Wanda had only replaced it once. The battery's sole task was to move two delicate, black hands, with gentle twitches, around the blue ceramic clock, and that task, evidently, required very little energy.

Wanda wished she had fewer tasks. She felt as if moving through her life her life required a huge battery, heavy and dangerous. She glanced up at the clock many times throughout the day, for reassurance, mainly.

MERLIN AND THE CARDINAL

RUSHING FROM THE KITCHEN, LEAVING the gravy to curdle on the stove, Wanda joined her family gathered in front of the creche on the wide window ledge in the dining room. No one was paying attention to the Christmas miracle. Instead they were mesmerized by the drama outside.

Wanda returned to the kitchen. She gave the gravy a desultory swipe with the whisk and poured it into the gravy boat, lumps and all.

The younger of her grandsons trailed into the kitchen. Wanda picked him up and kissed the tip of his nose.

"My chair," he demanded.

"Please?" Wanda prompted.

"Please," he responded agreeably.

Wanda set him down and carried his high chair into the dining room.

"Dinner?" she inquired of the assortment of backs still looking out the window. The older of her grandsons turned around.

"The bird flew away," he announced. "Both birds," he added. "I'm hungry," he finished.

Wanda, kneeling in front of him, felt the fierceness of his hug.

"Time to eat," she agreed, remembering just in time that he disliked being kissed on the top of his head.

Wanda fixed plates for her grandsons while her son-in-law droned on about the predatory habits of falcons.

When they were finally all seated around the table, hands joined, Wanda improvised a blessing. "Bless this food and the hope that's born on Christmas Day," she said.

"Amen," the adults agreed, their attention fixed on the food heaped on their plates.

"And the red bird," Wanda's older grandson added.

"Yes, and the red bird," Wanda agreed.

"That red bird is a cardinal," Wanda's husband told her older grandson as forks clinked against china.

"Why is it called a cardinal?" Wanda's older grandson asked him.

"Well," her husband improvised, "He's like men who think they can be the boss of how you talk to God. Those men dress up in bright, red robes and call themselves cardinals."

Wanda was relieved to see that her cousin, rather particular in matters of theology and child rearing, was politely listening to an uncle at the far end of the table.

"Did the red bird in the yard think he could boss the other birds around?" Wanda's older grandson asked her husband.

"He did," Wanda's husband said, "So Merlin came to teach him a lesson."

"Is that the name of the other bird?" Wanda's grandson asked.

"It is," Wanda's husband asserted. "He's a magician. That's why he came to our yard on Christmas day."

Wanda glanced anxiously at her cousin.

"Why Christmas?" Wanda's older grandson asked. Her younger grandson was listening now too.

"Well," Wanda's husband hedged uneasily.

"What's special about this day, besides Santa Claus?" Wanda asked her older grandson, buying her husband some time.

"It's that baby's birthday," he answered, pointing at the creche.

Wanda watched her husband rediscover the thread of his story.

"Right. Lots of people came to visit him. Including magicians we call Wise Men," her husband said.

"Are they the ones who followed the star?"

"Yes."

Wanda's older grandson chewed a bite of turkey while her younger grandson blew bubbles in his milk with his red straw.

"They saw a star that was so bright they knew they'd better follow it," Wanda's older grandson said after he swallowed his mouthful of turkey.

Into the sudden silence that sometimes punctuates all the dinner conversations up and down a table, Wanda's younger grandson stopped blowing bubbles and began his favorite song:

> Twinkle, twinkle little star,
> How I wonder what you are.
> Up above the world so high
> Like a diamond in the sky.
> Twinkle, twinkle, little, tiny star,
> How I wonder what you are.

All the adults, and Wanda's older grandson, gave him a round of applause. Then it was time to clear the table.

That night, as they sat reading in bed, Wanda and her husband were quiet for a while.

"Listen to this," her husband said, reading from the book he borrowed from their son-in-law at the end of the evening.

"Our Merlin is usually silent and seemingly heartless. I like 'seemingly heartless,' don't you? Pretty poetic for a reference book."

In response Wanda read,

>Hope is the thing with feathers
>That perches in the soul,
>And sings the tune without the words
>And never stops at all.

Then, the day's mysteries acknowledged, they turned off their bed-side reading lamps and reached for each other as stars twinkled in the cold December sky.

MOVE

Wanda realized she could, finally, make the move.

For seven years she woke each morning in the guest bedroom. For seven years she availed herself of the hall bathroom. For seven years she followed the uncovered, uneven path to her studio.

The studio had no heat or water. Snakes molted behind the bookcase. Toads hopped across the floor. Water stains decorated one corner, and part of the ceiling buckled ominously whenever it rained.

Even when it rained or hailed or snowed, or was freezing cold or stiflingly hot in Wanda's studio, Wanda's husband frowned if he left his study and saw Wanda and her laptop at the kitchen counter or the dining room table.

But still, it was her impregnable world.

Until Wanda noticed a man standing outside the fence below her studio. He was smoking a cigarette and staring at Wanda as she tottered in a balance pose on the other side of the studio's wall of windows.

Wanda collapsed onto her mat and curled up into a hedgehog. She counted slowly to five hundred and then peered over the window ledge. The man was gone. For now.

Wanda minded. That and other things.

Her husband minded other things about Wanda too.

Her husband packed up and left.

Wanda moved her clothes from the cramped guest-room closet

to the spacious dressing room. She moved her toiletries and towels into the master bathroom and soaked in the tub and steamed in the shower. She moved her paintings from their exile in the studio and hung them on the master bedroom's walls. (One was too damaged by damp to save.) Wanda washed the bedding for the king-size bed in the master bedroom and smudged the room with sage. She hung curtains over the master bedroom's sliding glass doors and the study's window.

Once Wanda even took a nap on the king-size bed.

But each night she slept in her four-poster bed in the guest bedroom.

Each morning she walked past the hall bathroom and through the master bedroom and dressing room into the master bathroom where she brushed her teeth and washed her face and sometimes showered. She dressed in the dressing room and then returned to the guest bedroom and made the bed.

Until one night she realized she was tired of making and keeping her life so complicated.

Wanda turned on all the lights in the master bedroom and tugged and shoved the king-size bed to the opposite wall.

Wanda went to the kitchen and assembled a tuna sandwich. She peeled and ate a carrot and garnished her plate with a pretzel. Wanda took her plate and a bottle of beer into the living room. She pushed buttons on the remote until Netflix appeared. She ate her sandwich and her pretzel and drank her beer. Then she tidied up the house and brushed her teeth and fetched her nightgown from the guest bedroom closet and her pillows from the guest bedroom bed and crawled between her husband's sheets—they smelled like smudging sage, not him—and lay her head on her own pillow and waited for sleep, or whatever the night and her future might bring.

In the morning, when Wanda opened the curtains, she could see her studio as she drank her coffee in bed. She could watch whatever weather was happening along the studio's path as if she were watching a movie or a TV weather video.

NEW YEAR'S EVE

WANDA HAD THE ENERGIZED, CARPE-DIEM feeling that grows from more than one generous pour of a different, more expensive red than the daily table fare. A thought nibbled daintily but persistently, consuming a hole in her enjoyment. Could it be three glasses?

Wanda snuggled closer on the faux leather loveseat. The two-seater. 2=2. That was the philosophy, the emotional heave-ho, of this man to her right.

The movie caught her attention for a moment.

Darcy was woodenly steering Elizabeth Bennett around a dance floor. Would his money, his considerable fortune, grease the equal sign and ease the marital equation? What happened after the wedding?

Wanda once wanted her marital equation to expand into something new. A family.

2=2 becomes 3=2+1 becomes 4=2+1+1, etc.

Wanda's husband was bad at arithmetic. For him 3=2-1, etc. Wanda as mother wasn't Wanda as wife. Love was finite. Love was choice.

Wanda recently proposed buying a duplex. She imagined two identical doors, mossy green maybe, offering two entrances into a sturdy brick house. (She and her husband had become practical little pigs after decades rebuilding straw and sticks.) A duplex for two retirees possessed of two modest retirement incomes (though her husband's was less modest) and two health care policies covering both pre-existing conditions and undreamed of catastrophes.

Which side would be hers? They recently switched sleeping sides, part of a campaign to avert Alzheimer's by altering routines. Each was now a brave little soldier steadfastly remaining on unfamiliar terrain during the strange, unconscious world of sleep that beckoned more and more as a plausible final destination.

Though neither had been sleeping well. He stayed up later and later, only falling into a deep sleep when Wanda got up, earlier and earlier, to feed the cats and exercise and putter in the kitchen.

Wanda drifted back to the movie. Darcy was smiling at Elizabeth. Love and lucre with, Wanda mused hopefully, a dose of lust thrown in, awaited the consummation so gracelessly foreshadowed by Lydia's unfortunate elopement.

Wanda stood up and returned the hug that faced her in the early new year.

NUPTIALS

THE PHONE RANG. WANDA, STRUGGLING into panty hose, glanced at the man. He was gleaming in front of the full-length mirror on the hotel room door, regal in cutaway and top hat. Clearly the phone hadn't ruffled the surface of his self-absorption.

Molly's voice, coming to Wanda from a room two floors above them, sounded calm and commanding. "You may come up now, Mom. Dad too, if he wants."

Wanda hopped over to the cutaway and top hat. "We're supposed to go up now," she said.

"I'll be ready in a few minutes," her husband replied.

Wanda hopped back to the bed and sat on the edge, reminding herself to breathe. The venerable hotel's overpriced atmosphere was perfumed by aging carpet and curtains and a miasma of persistent cigarette smoke and dust.

Wanda stood up and contorted her thighs, abdomen and buttocks into the restraint system of synthetic fibers that would bully her mother-of-the -bride dress into draping, not clinging. Molly detested any form of clinging.

The curling iron, heating up on the discolored bathroom vanity, glowered at Wanda. Avoiding her image in the mirror, Wanda yanked the plug out of the socket. Molly was waiting.

Wanda grabbed her hotel key, the unfamiliar satin purse, and a virginal tube of lipstick.

"I'll be up soon," her husband smiled as he stepped aside so she could leave.

For once, Wanda ignored her mother's admonition against applying make-up in public. As the elevator lurched upward, she smeared an approximation of her mouth with the lipstick Molly had chosen. She put the now-ravished tube in the satin purse just as the elevator jolted to a stop at the fifth floor. While butterflies collided below her heart, Wanda tottered out of the elevator on stiletto heels. Molly, who towered over Wanda on athletic, shapely legs, would be wearing, Wanda knew, white satin flats.

"This is a big day for you, too," Molly had explained when she chose Wanda's heels. "I want everyone to notice you."

The bunion on Wanda's right foot screamed its agony as she followed a starched shirt-and-tie businessman down the corridor. Wanda wondered if she should invite him to the wedding. What other excuse could there be for such sartorial misery on a Saturday morning?

Molly opened the door before Wanda even knocked. She beamed her benediction.

"We're beautiful, Mom."

PALE ZINNIA

WANDA CONTEMPLATED HER FLOWER ARRANGEMENT, the one she assembled two days ago, when her sister died.

Zinnias. Bold magentas and crimsons. Like her sister.

Already their stems were beginning to sag, their edges brown. She propped the zinnias against the side of the sink and poured the smell of decay down the drain.

Wanda's sister changed the water in her flower arrangements each day. She kept her circle of friends fresh too, by cultivating new acquaintances. Her house was always full of fresh flowers and people.

As Wanda carried the bunch of zinnias to the compost pile, she noticed that one pale pink flower still looked sprightly.

After trimming its sturdy stem at a sharp diagonal, she made room for the quiet zinnia in a new arrangement of her sister's bold, brief colors.

PENSIVE

WANDA'S BROTHER PAINTED PICTURES BASED on old photographs, some from family albums, some from friends and antique stores. He didn't copy the photos verbatim, or whatever passes for verbatim in the world of images. Instead he captured the mood and the implied narrative, to him at least, among the people in the photographs, or, in the case of portraits, the relationship between the persona of the sitter and the life below the surface.

Equally compelling to her brother, in the photographs that served as his muse, was the setting. He edited the setting to suit his narrative. A car became a truck. A dog was negative space. A cloud became a hot air balloon.

Over the decades Wanda acquired several of her brother's paintings, sometimes gifts, sometimes purchased cheaply, and once, in the context of Wanda's modest budget for aesthetic satisfaction, for a lot of money.

One—it was purchased cheaply, on a whim, in an art gallery— was a woman sitting on a stone wall contemplating an ambiguous landscape. Her brother once told her what the landscape was, but Wanda immediately forgot. The patches of fluffy whiteness could be snow or choppy waves. Wanda could edit the setting too, like her brother, according to narrative need.

The woman was dressed in black like the French Lieutenant's Woman in the novel by that name. Wanda read the book in her twenties. She had forgotten the plot but remembered the woman.

Whether the woman in the painting was enjoying her solitude or felt lonely Wanda didn't know. But she was, for sure, pensive.

Wanda's father, whenever he caught her sitting by herself without a book or other evidence of occupation, always asked her why she was so pensive. Wanda experienced this as a rebuke. Don't just be. Do something, anything!

Wanda had never pursued an exact definition of pensive. But she knew that, for people like her father, it had negative connotations.

What Wanda most liked about her pensive painting was the woman's smile. It was not a selfie-smile, all perfect teeth and smug assurance but, rather, a self-contained smile, one the Virgin might have worn when she learned she was to be the mother of God and, pensively, set aside her book.

RED-LETTER DAYS

WANDA'S OPENED HER ONLINE *Great Courses* tour of The Middle Ages, a thoughtful birthday gift from her antiquarian brother. Today's topic was "Illuminated Books of Hours".

Each Book of Hours was unique, the lecturer said. You could tell a lot about each unique book, and its patron, the lecturer added, by the red-letter days in its calendar. Each Book of Hours' red letters were unique to the place and time and sensibility of the person who paid for its creation, and to some extent, the lecturer added, to the preferences of the scribe and illustrator.

Wanda liked the personal preferences aspect of these medieval calendars. The truth was there she believed. Her own imagination had red-letter days that skirted birthdays and Christmas and national holidays that closed the postal service and public schools.

Yesterday was one of those days.

Wanda was, as usual, sleep deprived. But she had promised a masked and distanced visit with a friend who sounded desperate.

A double-espresso guided her car to her friend's driveway. Her friend greeted Wanda, arms outstretched, with a package wrapped in red paper and tied with a red ribbon. Wanda outstretched her own arms for a safe transfer and put the package in her car, on the floor, where the coronavirus wouldn't shed on her car's upholstery. She felt a bit grumpy about this early Christmas present. They always exchanged presents, but Wanda wasn't doing presents this year.

When Wanda drove home, she stopped at her rural mailbox.

There was a small, neatly taped package from a West Coast friend. Wanda hoped it was random, not holiday focused.

Wanda carried the red package and the Priority Mail package to the laundry room where they could companionably shed Covid for a while. She went in the bathroom and washed her hands to "Happy Birthday to Me" sung twice. Then she retrieved her phone from the pocket of her coat and settled herself on the porch hammock to read a lengthy text.

There was an enthusiastic knocking at the front door. Wanda had decommissioned the front door. No one was welcome in her house during the pandemic.

Wanda carefully positioned a mask that was airing on the screen porch. She waved through the porch screen door at her neighbor at the front door and joined her, at a distance. Her neighbor put a bag brimming with holiday wrappings on the chair by Wanda's front door. The bag was red, like her neighbor's mask.

That night Wanda wrote in her journal, Today was a red-letter day.

RULES

Wanda was a fan of rules. One cup of coffee. One glass of wine. Yoga every other day. Two walks a day. Never miss a wedding.

But Wanda had missed a wedding of the child of a friend.

Wanda blamed the infraction, along with everything else she found upsetting about her current situation, on her husband. Going to a wedding, when married, involved going to the wedding as a married couple, a stalwart example of why the institution was of value and worth undertaking. Wanda no longer believed in either the institution or the undertaking.

Like everything else she pondered in the murky present, Wanda found a precedent in the past. She remembered buying a wedding gift for a friend who was, to their shared befuddlement—Wanda's and her husband's—marrying his young student, a woman barely older than his son. Nonetheless, Wanda went to the mall for a present, wrapped it, and prepared to change her clothes.

At which time, her husband announced that he was leaving for the wedding at that very minute, that he wouldn't delay his departure to accommodate Wanda's schedule.

Wanda lacked the time to extricate the cause of his displeasure or to placate his sudden shift of mood. He was gone.

The wedding was in a distant, obscure corner of their sprawling county. Wanda doggedly channeled her fury into decisive action and arrived just before the bride made her entrance. Her husband grudgingly moved over for Wanda. They maintained a careful, cold distance throughout the service.

RUNNING ON EMPTY

Wanda woke up, glanced at the bedside clock, and turned on the bedside lamp to confirm. Yes! She had slept straight through to 6 AM. A day fueled by sleep, the insomniac's fantasy, beckoned seductively.

However, Wanda thought, blurry with a backlog of sleepless nights, complacent people who go to sleep, routinely, when they go to bed, have a functional baseline that's hard not to envy.

Wanda remembered her father, red-eyed from the anxiety that kept him tossing all night, and wondered if her brain, too, was being nibbled away, night after night, by the wear and tear of no sleep.

Which began when she was fourteen. Early-onset insomnia. Wanda's mother requested pills from a family friend who happened to be a doctor, sleeping pills and tranquilizers.

The family friend wanted to delay pills, he confided to Wanda as he perched on the edge of her bed holding one of her warty hands, until the unpleasantness of burning the warts was behind them. He wanted them to be friends so she could tell him how the sleeping and tranquility were progressing.

Wanda wondered how a person was supposed to sleep when a family friend, quite tipsy, could barge into your bedroom and sit on your bed. She decided that she'd stick with insomnia until she had a home of her own, safe and peaceful.

A barrage of laughter shot through the floor from the living room below Wanda's bed. The family friend stood up, leaned over Wanda to kiss her forehead, and departed.

It used to be her father arriving, unannounced, to tuck her in. Wanda had the vigilance of a sniper, without the sniper's rifle.

Often Wanda lay awake as the hours passed by, the molecules racing around her body. Finally the sky would start to brighten. She felt hopeful until she got up and realized there was a day to be traveled with nothing in the fuel tank. She'd just have to get out and push.

But today she had sleep. The gauge was above empty, maybe a quarter of a tank.

Wanda got up and went into the kitchen to start the coffee. From the deck outside the kitchen she watched the world slowly wake up with her. Pink streaked the sky. An unkempt bush's pink flowers scented the air. Wanda laughed out loud. She hated the color pink.

The coffee finished dripping. Wanda filled her mug and sat on her favorite bench, waiting for the rabbits to wake up and begin nibbling her garden.

SILENT READING

WANDA WAS GLAD HER SCREEN was turned away from her students. Unless one of them risked hellfire and damnation by coming to her desk during Silent Reading Time, Wanda could worry the ugly email from Principal Daniels for five more minutes.

Silent Spring by Rachel Carson, a long-ago Christmas present from her mother, was open on her desk. Wanda planned to use it as part of her Climate Change unit. But right now she couldn't focus on the harbinger of DDT.

"The name(s) of any student(s) who should be retained in third grade must be sent to me by 3:00 PM today."

Wanda accidentally caught Clifton's eye. He held up *Frog and Toad* and shot her a triumphant grin. Wanda grinned back.

Damn. Principal Daniels didn't care that Clifton was reading eagerly now. She wasn't interested that he hadn't been thrown off the bus for fighting since January or that he hadn't kicked anyone during recess for almost two weeks. Principal Daniels only cared that Clifton was reading below grade level and would, therefore, most certainly lower the overall achievement of third graders at her School of Excellence. Following the bureaucratic logic of "No child Left Behind," Clifton must be left behind. He certainly couldn't be allowed to progress to fourth grade where there were even more tests to showcase the excellence of Principal Daniels' school.

Wanda watched the top of Clifton's head as he bent over the book. During their reading conference yesterday, Clifton expressed his admiration for Toad's list that began "Get up" and ended "Go to sleep". Clifton thought it was a very good idea to have a list to guide you through your day. He loved the class schedule on the white board and volunteered to read it every day, now that he could read. If a frazzled Wanda, late to work because of a flat tire or a sick child, forgot to write down the bathroom break after recess or desk-clean-up time, Clifton's eyes would widen and fix on Wanda until she noticed the fissure she had created in his day and pulled him to safety by inserting, in very small but certain script, the activity that rescued his routine.

Principal Daniels assigned retained students to a different teacher. Her annual teacher evaluations noted each pedagogical failure to have a student clear all testing hurdles. Principal Daniels kept her eye on the finish line. She never noticed that the starting line was much further from the finish line for some students in her school.

Breaking her own rule, risking her own hellfire and damnation, Wanda walked over to Clifton's desk. Clifton was reading the chapter called "The Dream". Distracted by Wanda's presence, he pointed at her schedule on the board.

2:00 to 2:30 Silent Reading Stay in your seat.

Chastened, Wanda attempted a smile, which Clifton didn't return, and returned to her desk. Reviving the computer screen, she surreptitiously tapped out Clifton's name and the plea, "Request retention to current classroom."

The students stirred in their seats and turned their heads to Wanda.

"Time for the Multiplication Facts Relay Race," she announced with conviction.

Wanda felt the absolution of Clifton's smile.

SIAMESE FROGS

WANDA KNOCKED HER HIP WADERS against a rock to encourage the departure of hibernating creatures. Then she pulled each wader on and up and tightened the straps. Sitting on the rock she lowered herself into the pond and splashed enthusiastically, both to alert aquatic creatures of her whereabouts and for the sheer pleasure of splashing in a small pond in early spring with no audience but one plump frog hiding behind a fern. How could it already be so big and fat?

Wanda's new solitary dispensation made the happenings of each day peek or pop out unexpectedly, like delicious surprises, savory treats in succession, especially now that spring was here.

While she scooped up slimy twigs and acorns and tossed them into a bucket beside the pond, Wanda imagined herself fastening a screen across the pond's surface in the fall to eliminate this annual chore. She was scheming strategies to age in place; a despicable term, but still...

Then Wanda noticed piggyback frogs kicking their legs in unison.

At first she thought they were enjoying frog sex. But the frog on top had its front legs fused into the back of the frog on the bottom. How will they eat, Wanda wondered? How will they survive?

The Siamese frogs were the saddest thing Wanda had seen in the pond for the seven years she had been watching. They were sadder, even, than when the Blue Heron flew to the top of the chimney and perched there, gloating, before swooping down to eat the goldfish that survived the winter.

Wanda emailed a picture of the Siamese frogs to her used-to-be husband. She tried not to wonder what he'd think.

SNAKE SKIN

AT FIRST, FOR A YEAR or two, Wanda entered the studio nervously, feeling like an interloper in its light-drenched perfection. She missed the tiny studio in her former garden, the studio whose scale matched hers; it was too small for visitors. It was roughly finished inside, without insulation, but had gingerbread trim and a window box and a Dutch door, top and bottom. Wanda painted the outside three different colors and planted flowers all around. That's how she shared it with outsiders. But the inside was hers alone.

This new studio was spacious enough for visitors, but inhospitable. The furniture consisted of two chairs, one a torment to sit in, a long table, and a battered easel. No one but Wanda ever stayed long enough to take a seat. The occasional toad hopped in and, neglecting to hop out, shriveled up in a corner. A bird attempted the door and left a single feather stuck to the glass above its corpse. And each spring, during her annual sweeping and dusting, Wanda discovered the long, empty skin of a black snake.

Wanda was glad the studio lent itself to shedding skin that, like hers, had grown too tight and required privacy for shedding. However, she had recently sealed each crevice and crack around the door against her subtle reptilian shape shifter. The black snake had violated the studio's rules of consideration and tact when it pulled down the top of a poster by the door and coiled up in the poster's fold.

Wanda's surprised scream summoned her husband who,

chivalrously, assumed the role of St. George slaying the dragon to rescue the damsel in distress. Taking in the situation, he hurried away and returned with a hoe and a murderous gleam.

Wanda had no desire for vengeance. All she required was a studio free from external shocks and interruptions. From outsiders. Including knights. Wanda knew their rescuing was costly. Armor to polish. Lance to keep sharpened. Feast to celebrate valor.

However, she was glad for help in prodding the snake from the poster and gentling it out the door, she with a broom, her husband with encouragement.

After he and the snake left, Wanda tacked the Annunciation poster back into position. She wondered what inspired the black snake to be part of the picture.

SORTING SOCKS

IT DIDN'T RAIN AFTER ALL. No one twisted an ankle or bruised an ego. Wanda found it disconcerting to have her expectations thwarted by the amicability of both the weather and her family. And so, like an early Christian martyr who, escaping ravishment by a lion, indulged in the solace of self-flagellation, Wanda set herself to the task of sorting socks.

Wanda read somewhere that washing machines, when sufficiently agitated, eat socks. She found this insight into the workings of the mysterious physical world both consoling on a practical level and illuminating as a metaphor for her own spiritual aspirations. She liked the notion that random bits and pieces could disappear forever into the workings of some gigantic, mystical mechanism and transcend the smelly, functional, binary quality of her world.

Her family, however, perceived socks as tubular bits of cotton or wool that should unfailingly travel through life as matching pairs.

While Wanda shared her family's opinion that she didn't care if their socks matched, what she didn't share was their belief that she should care, that she was somehow morally flawed by her indifference to their socks (indeed to their feet, if it came to that). So sorting socks was a complex activity for Wanda. It both satisfied her sense of the way things really are, in the deep structure of the universe, and forced her to participate in social interactions that denied the validity of her metaphysical musings, as well as her existence.

"Good picnic, Mom. You didn't even drop the watermelon this

time. Dad wasn't too big of a jerk and Molly's bitch-from-hell routine didn't impress anyone."

Mark scooped up his pile of laundry from the quilt covering the matrimonial bed and headed out the master bedroom door.

Leaving the cat to choose which pile of laundry to tip over and sprinkle with dander, a bemused Wanda wandered out of the bedroom, barely registering the affront to her hip as she careened into the corner of a bureau that caught her at least once a day.

When much younger, Mark cut out footprints and taped them to the floor to describe a path of safety. Wanda had been touched by his concern and amused by his whimsy. Her body, however, had its own agenda and refused to focus on Mark's less perilous route. She found the permanent bruise on her hip a comforting reminder of her unsuitability for the mundane physical world.

The extended-family picnic had not been Wanda's idea. The concept of family had moved so far up Wanda's personal ladder of abstraction that she no longer tried to actualize it in the here and now. Family was enshrined for Wanda on some Platonic pedestal surrounded by puffy or wispy clouds, depending on her mood.

Wanda's sister, however, knew exactly how family should manifest and had the tenacity to forge her recalcitrant blood and marital attachments into rigid tableaux that conformed to her vision.

Wanda's sister was an artist. Her medium was canvas, but Wanda always suspected that marble would be a happier vehicle for her rendering of reality. Wanda felt the chisel and hammer hard at work, vigorously chipping away at any obdurate matter that tried to resist familial potential. Wanda imagined sneaking into her sister's studio each night to sweep up the chips and marble dust and glue gun them back in place. Each morning she'd discover the perfection she was liberating with her passionate blows safely back inside the cold, smooth, pristine block.

"Hi, Mom. Nice spot on your shirt. What's for dinner?"

Wanda felt herself instantly transformed into a box-like seventh grade science experiment, a battery-operated-push-button gadget with one simple circuit. The button having been pushed, she responded as she must.

"Molly, we don't all share your teflon-like capacity to move through the mire of life unblemished by mortal grime".

"True, Mom. But most of us past the age of six manage to get through the day without advertising what we had for lunch."

"Besides, Molly, why should I know, or even consider, what's for dinner? We just had a sybaritic picnic lunch surrounded by our loving extended family."

"Mom, as you would know if you consulted a mundane timepiece instead of your unique inner clock, it is now seven. Besides, your brothers are vegetarians and your sister's anorexic. Your contribution of a watermelon didn't exactly take up the slack.

I'm going to Tonya's."

The mixture of guilt and resentment engendered by this exchange was interrupted by Molly's affectionate, if condescending, pat on the head.

"I'm proud of you for not getting pulled down by all your sister's bullshit. Nice job, Mom."

The door slammed. The car's engine noisily turned over. Molly was gone, leaving a vacuum in the room.

"What's for dinner, Mom? If it's lentils again, I'm leaving."

"No, Mark. It's vipers, venom, and vexation."

"Right, Mom. See you later."

Another car pulled away.

Exaltation swept over Wanda. Dinner forestalled for another day. She meandered into the kitchen to the satisfying sight of her husband fixing himself a peanut butter and jelly sandwich.

"I need a hug," Wanda said.

"You've got it," was the satisfactory response.

"Did I survive?"

"You look pretty good. Where are the kids?"

"Gone."

"Excellent."

"I love you."

"I love you too."

"Want a carrot with your sandwich?"

"Sure."

Wanda peeled two carrots and joined her husband on the living room sofa. She muted a documentary, explaining the underpinnings of American foreign policy, with the satisfying crunch of her carrot. Maybe it wouldn't rain tomorrow either.

SUDOKU

Waking early, as usual, Wanda wandered into the spare bathroom and closed the door. She lowered the toilet seat cover—in this bathroom, at least, the toilet seat was always down—and pulled open the bottom drawer of the vanity where she stored the Sudoku puzzle book and the mechanical pencil under the monogrammed hand towels.

Wanda stared out the window at the darkness separating her from the time when she could clatter in the kitchen, making coffee and emptying the dishwasher, without disturbing her husband; he slept, unfailingly, until the sky brightened.

On the window sill was a sculpture of a boy drinking from a garden hose while peeing. It was Wanda's nod to the water cycle she taught in a science unit, year after year, to restless eight-year-olds. She imagined the little boy, in that implausible crouch peculiar to very young children, as a rain god ingesting clean, clear water from some suburban spigot and returning it to the earth as uric acid.

Wanda loved Sudoku. Though she knew it wasn't Japanese, it sounded as if it could be. Loving the puzzles compensated, in some small part, for her father's post-WWII hatred, undiminished into the 21st century, of all things Japanese.

Solving the puzzles also stood in for the certainties of the Baltimore Catechism, memorized while folding laundry with her mother. An older, orphaned Wanda had pivoted to Sudoku's clean, clear world of nine digits that must obey fixed rules in each new puzzle.

Unlike when she taught children, when a digit broke the rules, Wanda could eliminate its puzzle from her ongoing care and concern, marking it out with a large and definite X, turning the page and moving on. No need to wait for June and the retention, to a different classroom, of a child she failed to figure out, day after day. No need, in Sudoku, to take early retirement because of too many X's.

Dawn brightened the window sill. Wanda returned the Sudoku puzzle book and mechanical pencil to the drawer.

SWIMMING

WHEN WANDA WAS SIX, SHE came in first in a swimming competition at her parents' club.

It was Labor Day weekend. Wanda's parents and their friends watched from the shore as their children, tan and glowing from a summer of privileged beach days, kicked and flailed their way between ropes festooned with miniature red and white buoys.

When the race was over, the children swam to the shore to be congratulated or consoled by their parents while the older children competed. Then the swimmers ringed a platform with three pedestals, the middle one for the first-place winner in each age group. That lofty pedestal was, for a rare photo opportunity, Wanda's.

Wanda didn't pursue an Olympian path to further swimming triumphs. She didn't frame herself as a champion swimmer. She just swam whenever the opportunity presented itself:in oceans and lakes and creeks and quarries, and swimming pools in a pinch, often by herself.

Wanda's sister came to swimming late, swimming as a passion that is. Swimming didn't become an essential building block of life for Wanda's sister until she left her husband on their landlocked farm and moved to a fisherman's cottage by the sea. She became an eccentric swimmer in her new world and life, a woman of a certain age who swam in all seasons and against all warnings of rip tide and pollution. She swam until, for the last time, maneuvered from wheel chair to flotation tube, she paddled her hands in the water and stared at the clouds and sky.

After her sister died, Wanda wore her glasses when she swam so she could see the snapping turtles' heads popping up through the lake's surface. Even swimming felt perilous.

TEETER TOTTER

BALANCE THE TEETER TOTTER OR there will be the devil to pay, the Jungian lecturer intoned.

Wanda remembered the teeter totter on her kindergarten playground, back in the fifties, before seat belts and bicycle helmets. With nuclear apocalypse imminent, injuries and accidents seemed beside the point. Safety only existed for the few, in a backyard bomb shelter. The rest of the population had to make do with anxiety spiked by periodic drills: "Get under your desk with your hands over your head, children, when the siren signals the end of the world."

Wanda could still feel the spine-jarring impact when her end of the see saw plummeted to the concrete playground pavement. She could still see the malevolent grin of her classmate as he scooted to the middle of the seesaw to end their soothing rhythm of up and down.

The Jungian analyst was offering teeter totter examples. Balance acts of kindness with cruel journal entries; propriety out in the world with solitary, naked, frenzied dancing to Stravinsky's *Rites of Spring,* behind closed doors.

The list went on, but Wanda remained trapped by the image of the tall, sober, cerebral analyst in a naked dance.

Back in the dormitory room that was hers for the duration of the conference, beer in one hand, cigarette in the other, she despised the demarcation of inner/outer, good/bad, Apollonian/Dionysian.

She loathed the notion of the middle way, middle C, a neutral color palate.

What Wanda wanted, or wanted to want, was to run with the unbridled passion of her inner life, or what her inner life would be would be if she gave her imagination free rein.

Wanda poured the rest of the beer into the toilet and flushed. Then she flushed the cigarette stub too and cracked the window to air the room.

TICK

WANDA WOKE AT 12:01 AM. She read the news on her laptop. She finished reading *The New Yorker*, page by page. She turned off the bedside lamp and listened to a meditation tape on her new, alien Android. But sleep would not come.

Wanda wasn't worrying about Molly, even though it was Molly's birthday. Wanda wasn't suffering the itch of her self-imposed virginity.

But she was feeling an itch.

In the spirit of scientific discovery, Wanda cautiously explored her tangled thatch, thinning and graying but still capable of camouflage. She parted the wiry hairs and felt a bump on the front of her sex. Knowing, while refusing the knowledge, Wanda turned on the lamp and adjusted her glasses. Once again she journeyed her fingers to the unwelcome bump, the first visit in the calendar year from her nemesis:plump and with a white dot in the middle.

Her fingers more expert at this maneuver than the most surgical of tweezers, Wanda firmly grasped the base of the invader and gave a decisive tug. The tick continued to contentedly suck her blood and inject its pathogens into her bloodstream.

Wanda's mental eye scanned the medicine cabinet for her Official Tick Remover and found it on the second shelf next to the rubbing alcohol and tweezers. But experience reminded her that it only worked on ticks more conveniently located than this one. She reconsidered the more traditional alcohol and tweezers but, tired, grumpy, and contrarian, reverted to manual dexterity and perseverance.

Tick finally in hand and no longer enjoying its midnight snack, Wanda groaned herself out of bed, shuffled through the darkened house to the kitchen drawer, and felt around until she located the Scotch tape, actually the Dollar Store brand. Blindly, she affixed the tick, imagining its tiny legs dancing in protest, to the sticky side of the tape and waited for a moment as it began its impotent journey to death. Was it conscious of this unfortunate state of affairs? Wanda neither knew nor cared. She set the tick and tape on the counter and washed her hands at the kitchen sink, muscle memory guiding her in the dark. Then she shuffled back to bed to wait for dawn.

WELL

WANDA WANTED HER HOME TO be welcoming; she baked blueberry muffins for her friend who came to tea. Then they walked to the creek. The visit was a success.

The post-visit sink was full of bowls and measuring cups and the crusty muffin tin. Wanda turned on the faucet and reached for the dish detergent. She absentmindedly squeezed a generous squirt of detergent into the sink. She replaced the detergent bottle beside the faucet.

Something was amiss. Wanda focused on the sink. Then on the faucet.

No water.

Wanda sighed. She went to the circuit breaker and opened the door. The numbers beside each switch had grown smaller since Wanda last looked at them. Wanda went to the desk for the magnifying glass and to the pantry for a flashlight. The well was on circuit #3. The circuit had not tripped. None of the circuits had tripped.

Wanda checked the odd, mysterious outlet in the laundry room that went wonky from time to time. The green light was on.

She unlocked the studio and crawled over her husband's possessions. The circuit breaker outlet in the studio was in the farthest and most thoroughly barricaded corner. Wanda clambered over a grill and lawn furniture and her husband's beloved chain saw. She lay on her stomach on his bureau and contemplated three boxes between her and a sightline to the studio's circuit breaker. Wanda slithered into an impossibly narrow opening between the boxes and the bureaus. She lifted one box at a time onto the bureau. She plugged her emergency flashlight into the outlet. The light turned on. Wanda eyed the path back to the door and realized that a mishap in the studio wouldn't be discovered until her husband eventually reappeared to reclaim his stuff.

"Steady," she muttered. "Focus," she intoned.

Back at the house, Wanda filled the electric kettle with a gallon of bottled water; she kept six for emergencies.

While her tea steeped, she reminisced.

Wanda couldn't reach the cord that pulled down the ladder to the attic in their new home. She cajoled her husband to pull down the trap door and clambered ahead of him into the attic space. Together they contemplated a contraption that mediated solar back-up power; she sighed and he shrugged. "Sufficient unto the day?" Wanda suggested. Wanda and her husband hooked pinkies, signifying their accord on this matter.

Some days after, the water stopped. Just like that, no water came from a faucet.

The sky was blue. The air was calm. The electricity was flowing cheerfully everywhere except to the well. The well's circuit breaker hadn't tripped.

Wanda called the company that installed the pump. (The previous owners had left files so copious it was hard to locate that specific number. But, finally, Wanda did.)

Later that day a truck pulled into the driveway. A man surveyed the situation. He kindly, but a little smugly, told Wanda and her husband that the well was switched to solar power, and the battery had died. He reminded them of a week of cloudy weather that preceded this day of blue sky and sunshine. He muttered about the limitations of solar power and green energy. Then he flipped a switch in the bedroom closet. The closet was chock-a-block full of panels and gizmos related to the sole solar panel on the roof and the ominous battery in the attic. He walked to the kitchen and turned on the faucet. Water obediently streamed into the sink.

Wanda's husband went to get the household expenses checkbook. Wanda thanked the well man.

Neither Wanda nor her husband gave the well a practical thought for the next seven years. As she always had, Wanda kept bottled water on hand and filled containers with water at the first hint of weather mayhem. (Her husband wasn't proactive in this way. He didn't need to be because Wanda was.)

Now, seven years later, Wanda wondered if mechanical objects like pumps had some animus towards a woman who ended her marriage for reasons of the heart. Not the mechanical pump; rather the emotional heart that breaks, finally, after years of stress fractures. But that's bones.

She located the file folder labelled, unambiguously, *well,* and dialed the number she wrote with a bold indelible sharpie seven years ago.

On the phone the well man had lost none of his volubility. He was buried in his Christian volunteer activities. He lived forty minutes away. He was tired. It was Friday. He'd come on Monday.

When he arrived, late, he surveyed Wanda and the situation. He asked if she lived alone. Wanda allowed as how she did but offered up her son, just down the road, to show she was solitary but invulnerable. (She didn't tell the well man that hell would freeze over before she'd bother her busy son with her domestic challenges. She recently banished his dad. That was enough maternal trouble to cause for now.)

The well man suggested she try apartment living. Wanda

suggested he go under the house. The well man complained about spiders. Wanda handed him a broom. The well man shouted from under the house that her pump was 115 volts, not the standard 230. Wanda reminded him that she told him that on the phone. He mentioned it seven years ago. She wrote it down. The well man asked if the pump was still attached to the solar panel on the roof. Wanda repeated the conversation she had with him on the phone three days ago. The well man shouted from another position under the house.

"Here we go," he yelled cheerfully.

The well man crawled out from under the house and joined Wanda on the steps that led up to the deck. He said she had water again, but it wouldn't last long. She needed a new pump. He didn't have the pump she needed on his truck.

Wanda asked how much the new pump would cost. She confided that her heat pump just broke and her car needed a new clutch.

The well man said that at her age she should have saved enough for emergencies. Wanda told the well man that she did, but an enormous emergency wiped out her savings. (She didn't confide that the emergency was buying her husband's share of the house with its broken well.)

Wanda knew that the well man believed in the sanctity of Wanda's marriage. Wanda didn't feel confident in her counter arguments, but she was hoping for a modicum of pity and invoice adjustment.

The well man looked up at the blue sky and settled into the mid-afternoon warmth on Wanda's steps.

"Nice place you have here," he observed.

WEDDING

Are you excited about tomorrow?" asked Wanda's granddaughter.

"Not really," said Wanda. "I am curious though."

"What are you curious about?" asked her granddaughter.

"I'm curious about whether it's a good idea to be getting married."

"Well, I guess you'll find out," said her granddaughter.

"I guess I will," said Wanda.

"Are you going to wear flowers in your hair?" asked her granddaughter. "Like last time?"

"I wasn't planning to," Wanda answered.

"Well you should," said her granddaughter. "Only this time they should be real."

Wanda recalled the crown of tasteful fake flowers fastened to her long-ago wedding veil.

"Will you pick them for me?" Wanda asked.

Her granddaughter pondered this request. "I will," she decided. "But just one."

"What one will it be?" Wanda asked.

"I don't know, yet," said her granddaughter. "Tomorrow morning I'll pick the most beautiful daylily and put it in your hair."

"Right," said Wanda. "Thank you," she added.

END NOTES

A medieval Book of Hours was devoted to the Virgin Mary and offered eight daily opportunities, from Matins to Compline, for its owner to retreat from the world for prayer and contemplation.

Jeanne d'Evreux's Book of Hours pairs the Virgin's story with sorrowful episodes from the life of her Son. Visual humor throughout the book serves to divert and enrich the reader's experience.

The Metropolitan Museum of Art first published a facsimile of portions of *The Hours of Jeanne d'Evreux* in 1957.

"Zero" by Imagine Dragons plays during the credits of Disney's *Ralph Breaks the Internet*.